Now and Forever

by J.R. Zimmer

Book two
Fisher/Lafayette Saga

Badlanders Press

Now and Forever

©2020 by Janette Walker

Edited by Julie Baltzell

Cover design by Janette Walker

Model Image Credit:(c) gijones www.fotosearch.com.

ISBN 978-1-7345789-9-7

Cover design by Janette Walker

Fisher/Lafayette Saga

If There Hadn't Been You

Now and Forever

Someone Like You

Spitfire

Something Magical

Coming Home (Free Ebook when signing up for my newsletter at www.jrzimmer.com. Not available anywhere else)

The Dreamer

Eagle's Wolf

For

My Aunt and Uncle

Sharren and Charles Goehring

Thank you for always believing in me.

Now and Forever

by J.R. Zimmer

Prelude

Paris, France 1965

It was her birthday. Her twenty-seventh birthday, to be exact. As always, her parents planned a grand party for their only daughter and held the event at the family home. A medieval-styled, 18-bedroom Chateau west of Paris. It sat on 30 acres, and included a stable for horses, a small lake, and several outbuildings surrounding the home, all of which had a view of breathtaking landscapes.

Rosalinda was of French, Spanish, and Italian descent. She had always known wealth and luxury. Her second great grandfather, Richard, Duc de Vallombrosa, had founded the Yacht Club of France, and the Society of Racing, in Cannes. Before that, at twenty-two years of age, he led an expedition across India and earned the Cross of the Commander of the Or-der of St. Maurice and St. Lazare.

Richard Vallombrosa had married Geneviève de Pérusse des Cars, the daughter of the Duc de Cars, who had been one of the top commanders in the conquest of Algiers.

Despite their noble titles and wealth, Rosalinda's family was not aloof. Her parents taught their five children to have compassion for those who had not been fortunate enough to have riches of their own. They encouraged their children to give back whenever possible, whether it be volunteering at a local soup kitchen or donating to charities that offered assistance to the less fortunate.

That did not mean that Albert Vallombrosa and his wife were afraid to spend their money on outlandish parties. And this birthday bash for their youngest child would be the talk of the Paris elite society for a long time.

Rosalinda should have been having the time of her life. The musicians were one of France's most popular and famous groups. They sang and played their instruments on stage, and the people danced and laughed in the ballroom, enjoying the evening.

Among the guests were celebrities of film and the live theater. They were there to congratulate Rosalinda, who quickly rose in the ranks of popularity because of her exceptional acting abilities, as well as for winning the Best Actress award for her performance in the movie Love in The Spring last year.

However, Rosalinda was not enjoying herself and was not exactly sure why. Perhaps it was because she realized she was closer to thirty years of age than she would have liked to be. Or it could be she was saddened because her best friend, Jacqueline Fisher, could not attend the festivities. Even if Jacqueline wasn't pregnant, and scheduled to give birth in about a month, the woman would not have been able to attend; no longer able to travel freely to Paris. Because even though the woman's stepbrother thought she was dead, no one could take the chance that someone in France would recognize Jacqueline and report it to Pierre. He had hired a hitman to kill her three years ago and, as far as he knew, his directive had been successful.

Rosalinda's green eyes scanned the ever-increasing crowd. Until recently, she would have been scoping out a handsome man who would catch her fancy and then seduce him into a quick fuck. She'd always had a strong sexual drive and never wanted for willing partners who were happy to scratch her itch with no further demands or commitments.

But she was not interested in sex at the moment. At least, no one had struck her fancy or aroused sexual desires in her for the past four months.

Rosalinda wondered if something was wrong with her.

Her eyes went back to scanning the ever-growing crowd. What, or who, she was seeking; she wasn't certain.

She felt someone come up behind her. Turning, she found the American agent who helped escort Jacqueline's stepbrother to Fleury Mérogis prison three years ago, standing behind her. He was a handsome man, a

little over six feet tall, with a wide chest and muscular arms. Arms that held her a few times over the past three years. The first time she had gotten him into bed was the day she first met him. After that, he vowed it wouldn't happen again, and she'd viewed that as a challenge. The next time she saw him, at Colten and Jacqueline's wedding, she seduced him in his hotel room.

It had been a glorious night for both of them. So much so that each time he came to Paris, they would meet at her home and make memories, until it was time for him to catch the plane back to the United States.

Cadman Benson was a sexy-looking man and a superb lover. Yet, looking at him now, she had no interest in tearing his clothes off.

He smiled at her, that small dimple at the corner of his mouth she had always enjoyed sucking and licking peaked at her, and yet, tonight, it was nothing more to her than what it was. A dimple that was just there.

Obviously, she was coming down with something. Perhaps she should visit the doctor to find out if there was something wrong with her.

Cadman leaned in, kissed her cheek. "You are as beautiful as ever." When she made no move to make his kiss into anything more, it surprised him, but he shrugged it away. The on again, off again sexual relationship they shared satisfied him in ways no other woman could. Although he was half in love with her, he never fooled himself into thinking she would ever be his exclusively.

Besides, he was beginning a new career soon, for the United States government, which wouldn't leave him time to pursue any permanent relationship with anyone. And he was happy enough with the arrangement he had with Rosalinda.

"Thank you," she murmured, her eyes going back to the crowd.

"Are you looking for someone in particular?" Cadman asked, stepping up to stand beside her, as his eyes, too, scanned the crowd. He wondered if her indifference to him was because of her having her sights set on some other man tonight. Which actually bothered him. If she was looking for a sexual encounter, he was more than willing to be her slave.

"Umm?" Rosalinda's response wasn't an answer at all.

3

Shaking his head, he decided that whoever the starlet was searching for wasn't any of his business. He told her, "I'll be flying back to the United States tomorrow. Next month I'll be starting my vacation. I'm going to spend a week with Colten and Jacqueline in North Dakota, on that horse ranch of theirs."

Rosalinda glanced up at him and smiled. "I am jealous of you, Cadman. But I will travel there the moment Jacqueline sends word that the baby is born." She patted his arm. "Although I will miss seeing you ride a horse. The first time I witnessed it, I laughed for hours."

"Ha, ha," he said with a scowl. He hated horses, but every time he visited the Fisher ranch, which offered tourists a chance to horseback deeper into the Badlands of North Dakota, Colten somehow talked him into getting on one of those four-legged things he called a quarter horse.

Rosalinda's eyes moved to the entrance of the ballroom. They stopped when they landed on Charles Lafayette as he entered the room. The talented movie producer seemed to hesitate in the doorway for only a moment, before moving to where Rosalinda's parents stood next to the food table and refreshments.

Rosalinda's breath caught in her throat the instant she saw him enter the room, and she did not realize she was holding her breath until her lungs forced her to breathe.

The man was eleven years older than herself. She had used the age gap as an excuse for ignoring whatever feelings he evoked in her, but something seemed to be shifting inside her concerning him. Changes she wasn't sure if she wanted to admit.

A few months ago, she noticed he lost the small amount of extra weight he always carried around his stomach. And, although his balding head had some sections of hair trying to remain behind, it never distracted her from thinking he was attractive- and kind- and gallant. And why couldn't she allow herself to love him? She knew the man loved her. He showed her so many times over the years that he did not look at her as a sexual conquest and treated her as though he cherished her. He never suggested she sleep with him. Though Rosalinda saw the longing in his eyes whenever she caught him looking at her. She never tried to make

him a conquest; she respected him too much. And knew, too, that with him, he did not want a one-night stand. He would want more than she was ready to give one man.

He would want marriage and commitment.

Watching him now, speaking with her parents, she felt a familiar tug at her heart. She did not know what to do with these damn emotions that wanted to propel her to him.

As usual, he was alone. Rosalinda had never seen him with another woman, and her heart twisted. He deserved someone in his life who would understand he was worth loving.

In her eyes, he appeared lonely, and the urge to go to him was almost strong enough to cause her feet to move in his direction.

Ruthlessly, she pushed the desire down. She knew that if she went to Charles now, she would not want to let him go, and she was not ready to give up her freedom.

When the band played another number, she grabbed Cadman's hand and pulled him onto the dance floor, determined to forget about Charles Lafayette and the feelings his mere presence stirred within her.

Chapter One

One month later.

Charles Lafayette entered the restaurant, excited to know his vision of adding a backlot to his motion picture company would take place soon.

Over the past few years, his company gradually acquired neighboring land surrounding Lafayette Productions. As neighborhoods became abandoned or owners wanted to sell, they saw an opportunity for expansion. All that was left was for him to sign the paperwork drawn up by his lawyers. Once approved, that area would officially belong to him and his production company, completing the 26-acre expansion behind the studio. Then they could begin demolishing the neglected apartment buildings and houses that were long ago deserted and now in decay and ruin.

He preferred to shoot his films on location, but certain scenes were more practical to film on a backlot. There were others who required a larger space for their own productions and would pay whatever price he charged for its use.

Business was business, after all. His company was running in the black, and he would keep it that way if it were in his power to do so.

If there was one thing he could claim to be successful at, it was having the Midas touch in the movie industry.

He was worth millions.

His personal life, however, was another story. He was foolish enough to fall in love with a woman who would probably never return his affection. Although he told himself countless times to move on and find another woman, his heart would not comply. He tried to find interest in someone else to devote himself to, but to date, he encountered no one remarkable or captivating enough to give a second thought to.

He acknowledged he was a fool but could not change the fact he was old-fashioned. He was thirty-eight years old, and would no doubt die a lonely man.

Not that he hadn't experienced sex with a woman before.

During his college years, he occasionally took woman to bed. However, after meeting Rosalinda Vallombrosa, no other woman appealed to him.

The first time he saw her, he became smitten. She had been fifteen years old then. Far too young for him, but he had not thought of her sexually until she grew older.

Dominic, Rosalinda's brother and his former college classmate, made the introductions on opening night. It was at one of the many plays where she was developing her talent, and her gracefulness instantly drew him in.

The moment he saw her grace the stage for the first time, he knew Rosalinda was destined for stardom.

When Rosalinda turned seventeen, Charles cast her in a small part, in one of his first movies, and discovered how much the camera loved her.

Photographers were quick to notice how well Rosalinda could, virtually, have an affair with the lens of a camera. After that production, she quickly became one of the most sought-after women for modeling—just about anything.

At eighteen, she blossomed into a woman. That was when he knew he was in trouble with a capital T.

He tried to tell himself he was too old for her. But that did not mean his heart listened, and each time he heard the rumors of her many rendezvous and sexual encounters, his heart would feel as though it would break.

So many times, he'd wanted to invite her to share a meal with him, but he was afraid of rejection and ridiculed. So instead, he kept his feelings hidden. But did she not realize? Those men she slept with did not truly care for her. Did she not see she was worth so much more than being used for sexual pleasure?

While other men would grab her from behind, press their lips to hers, and make inappropriate comments, Charles was the complete opposite; he never laid a hand on her and always treated her with the utmost respect she deserved.

And it had gotten him nowhere, except to have an empty heart and broken dreams. Rosalinda appeared not to see him as a man whom she could love.

The restaurant was bustling with waitstaff taking and delivering orders; the maître d' directed the hostess like a conductor leading an orchestra. Across the busy room, Charles saw his lawyers and business partners, already seated at a long table near the back of the room.

When they spotted him, they waved him over.

Charles was just passing a table where an older woman, and possibly her daughter, sat enjoying their meal. Without warning, the younger woman pushed away from the table, stood up, and turned around.

She gave a startled squeal when she knocked into him. She would have fallen backward, had Charles not reached out to steady her.

"Oh!" the woman exclaimed, placing a hand to her heart. "I am so very sorry!"

Because her apology was spoken in English, he smoothly switched from French to address her in what seemed to be her native tongue.

"No harm done." He told her as his hand clasped her elbow to steady her. "Are you all right, mademoiselle?" he inquired.

"Yes!" she said, her voice sounding like a nervous laugh. "It was clumsy of me, not to look to see if anyone was behind me."

Charles regarded the attractive blonde. It surprised him he noticed her hair color, when the only color of hair to draw his attention over the past fifteen years was raven black.

He glanced at the woman sitting at the table and tried not to grimace. She reminded him of a skeleton with only enough skin on her body to cover the bones.

The blonde drew his attention back to her. "I am Aimée-Louise Fontaine," she motioned to the skull and bones on the other side of the table, "This is my mother, Lilith."

His manners had him doing a slight bow to the older woman. "It is nice to meet you. I am Charles Lafayette. Now, if you two ladies will please excuse me, I have a meet…."

Lilith smiled like a cat who'd unexpectedly discovered a bowl of fresh cream. "Charles Lafayette?" she questioned, calculating something only she understood. Her gaze shifted slyly towards her daughter before returning to the man in front of her. "Tell me," she said, with a hint of mischief in her voice, "you wouldn't be the same Charles Lafayette who owns Lafayette Productions, would you?"

"Yes," he acknowledged, then tried to say again, "Please excuse me," he motioned to the group of men waiting for him. "I have a meet…"

A sudden burst of excitement escaped Lilith. "Oh my goodness!" she exclaimed. Her gaze was locked on her daughter, attempting to transmit a message that only the two of them would understand. "Aimée-Louise, can you believe this incredible coincidence?"

Aimée-Louise expression as she gazed at her mother was one of disbelief and dread.

"Well?" Lilith's voice seemed to be conveying a message in that one word.

After a moment of hesitation, Aimée-Louise's gaze returned to Charles, forcing a smile onto her face. "Absolutely!" Her voice sounded strained. "It is wonderful to meet you. Would you care to take a seat?" She motioned toward the empty seat at the table which she was sharing with her mother.

"Ladies, please. I am here for a meeting."

Aimée-Louise exclaimed, "Oh, I'm so sorry! We didn't mean to interrupt your business. Since you can't join us tonight, we would be delighted to reschedule for dinner tomorrow evening."

Their audacity took him by surprise. Maybe it was because they were American; their English accents certainly hinted at it. Folks from that country didn't seem to possess the same etiquette as the French.

He shook his head and said, "I apologize, but I must take my leave." He couldn't help but add the obligatory phrase he learned from his childhood, "It was nice meeting you." Even though he didn't mean it. There was something about the mother that irked him, but he didn't bother to wait for her response or figure out what it was that bothered him. He simply turned and headed towards the table where his team of lawyers and colleagues were eagerly waiting for him.

Chapter Two

Charles made his usual Monday morning visit to the Louvre museum. He took pleasure in examining the masterpieces on display. The collections were so immense that he doubted he would ever be able to see every piece within the museum's walls.

He discovered a long ago that when he viewed the collections, his mind would clear. He would feel refreshed and inspired, allowing his own creativity and could face the demands put on him that week, whatever they may be. It was easier for him to choose a script or resolve how he wanted a scene in a film blocked after spending time at the world's largest art museum.

As usual, a bustling crowd of visitors filled the halls of the former royal palace this morning, where it now housed collections of Western art and displays from ancient civilizations. The sound of their voices bounced off the lofty walls as they mingled. Charles found himself wandering into one of the museum's many painting galleries, where the canvases were massive, some reaching up to twenty feet tall and thirty-two feet wide.

Some of his favorite paintings on display were La belle ferronnière, by Leonardo da Vinci, and the Grande and Odalisque by Jean Auguste Dominique Ingres. However, he liked more than only those few paintings hung in the room.

There were countless others he could name that also captured his attention.

Charles paused before the canvas titled "The Raft of the Medusa," painted by Théodore Géricault between 1818 and 1819. The massive oil painting, which was sixteen feet tall and twenty-three feet wide, depicted the harrowing scene of survivors and casualties from the 1816 shipwreck. The frigate, a 40-gun French Navy vessel called the Medusa, struck the Bank of Arguin due to inept navigation. It was a complete

11

loss, and tragically, only fifteen people survived out of four hundred passengers because there hadn't been enough lifeboats.

Charles's eyes roamed the canvas, always amazed by a painter's ability to create such lifelike renditions of the human body.

This painting had a raft in the center that filled most of the canvas. The raft, already broken, was being battered by the waves without mercy; the naked and half-clothed men holding on to whatever they could, to stay out of the water.

He stood there, viewing the masterpiece for almost a half-hour.

..After glancing at his watch, Charles decided to spend another half-hour at the museum before grabbing lunch and heading to the studio to handle his business paperwork.

He turned around, knowing that on the opposite wall was the portrait of the Charging Chasseur, painted in 1812 by Théodore Géricault.

Only a handful of people were examining the piece as he approached. To the right stood a couple, their hands clasped; a group of five gathered on the left. His attention fixed on a slim blonde woman in the center who seemed vaguely familiar. Between the dozens of daily interactions and the hundreds of faces he filmed, Charles couldn't place her, though the feeling of recognition persisted.

Ultimately, it made little a difference if he'd made her acquaintance before.

Charles stopped beside her, a few feet from her right.

If she knew him, she could say hello first.

No sooner had he begun viewing the Charging Chasseur, when he heard the woman say, "Oh my goodness, Mr. Lafayette! I can hardly believe I almost collided with you a few days ago, and now, by chance, here we are again."

..Turning toward her, Charles's memory clicked. With a jolt of surprise, he realized this familiar face belonged to the woman he had saved from a fall at the restaurant just a week ago.

He searched his memory for her name; trying to match one of the hundreds of names he knew to the woman's attractive face.

She rescued him by saying, "Aimée-Louise," as though she knew he was trying to remember the name she had given him Friday night.

"Ah, yes. It is nice to see you again." He spoke the words, though he wasn't entirely sincere. He found her presence here at the same time as his an odd coincidence, yet it might be nothing more.

She chuckled as she responded, "That's very sweet of you to say. I am afraid I did not make a good first impression." She glanced around the room. "Do you come to the Louvre often? This is my first time visiting Paris, as well as the museum. The artwork here is stunning, so I do not wish it to be my last."

"Yes, it is," he agreed, glancing around the space, looking for her mother. "Lilith, is not with you? Or is she viewing another section of the museum?" Why he suddenly thought of the ancient Egypt exhibit and the mummies there, he wasn't entirely certain. Regardless of the older woman reminding him of skin and bones, it had not been a charitable thought. No one asked to be born looking a certain way, and he was sorry he had had the unkind thought.

.."My mother instructed me to do this independently," Aimée-Louise explained, shrugging and then shook her head as though attempting to take back what she'd claimed. "But I truly am enjoying it. It's fascinating to study every brush stroke and wonder what the painter was thinking. Look at this horse, rearing away from some unseen threat. Is there an attacker, or is it simply hesitant to move?"

Charles couldn't help but smile, his face lighting up with excitement. "That is exactly what I have wondered while admiring this painting!" And before they knew it, they had moved on to discussing other works of art, dissecting brush strokes and deciphering symbolism.

Suddenly, Charles realized he had lost all track of time. He checked his watch and was stunned: two whole hours had vanished. Since he owned the production company, he had no one to answer to, but his pride in being punctual still made him worry about his late arrival at the office. The incredible truth was that he had been completely absorbed, enjoying Aimée-Louise's non-stop chatter and admiring her infectious smile.

..When the soft, familiar contours of Rosalinda's face momentarily broke through his focus, Charles responded by forcing himself to mentally block it. The image held only the bitter taste of something lost and irretrievable. Enough was enough. He forcefully reminded himself that it was time to stop hoping and to direct his considerable energy toward the tangible, and perhaps then find the companion he longed for.

The thought of a life without Rosalinda made his stomach turn, but the pain was quickly followed by a brutal dose of reality: she'd never truly been a part of his life, only a fleeting presence during the production of his movies.

Charles halted abruptly before Eugène Delacroix's "Women of Algiers." "Aimée-Louise," he began. He was surprised to hear the words leave his own mouth; he hadn't intended to linger with her, but the thought had jumped to an impulsive offer: "Would you be interested in joining me for lunch?"

The unexpected offer made Aimée-Louise gasp, her hand rising to her chest. "Mr. Lafayette," she said warmly, "I would be honored to join you for lunch. Thank you for your kindness."

"There is a wonderful place close by and within walking distance. And please, call me Charles."

She nodded. "All right…, Charles."

As they walked toward the eating establishment, Charles heard himself ask, "Should we invite your mother? I could have my driver pick her up." He immediately cursed the impeccable manners of his upbringing. Although he didn't know why, he wanted nothing to do with Aimée-Louise's mother and bitterly regretted having made the suggestion.

"No!" Aimée-Louise's face contorted as she closed her eyes for a moment, then composed herself with a deep breath. "I apologize. I did not intend for it to come out that way. What I meant was that she is currently visiting friends, and we are getting to know each other. She will be pleased to know that."

Relief made Charles smile, allowing him to relax with the realization there was no worry her mother would be joining them. "Perhaps another

time then," he said, knowing he didn't mean it in the slightest. He then motioned for Aimée-Louise to enter the restaurant.

The conversation was light during the meal. When asked, Aimée-Louise told him she and her mother were from New York state and that she had grown up in its capital city, Albany.

Charles was familiar with the location, as he owned a New York City home he occasionally visited for work trips overseas. The only other state he'd ever been to was California, specifically Hollywood. Because he always flew on his private jet, however, he had never bothered to learn the geography between the two states, and it mattered little to him.

His heart belonged to France.

"And what brings you to Paris?" he asked after the waiter took their order and scurried off to the kitchen to have it prepared.

Lifting the glass of water the waiter had set down before her, Aimée-Louise took a small sip, then another before saying, "It was my mother's idea. She thought it was best to leave…." Aimée-Louise coughed, excused herself, and began anew. "She thought it would be an excellent time of year to visit this beautiful city."

He couldn't help but notice her evident unease. which only amplified his earlier suspicion about her mother. Perhaps his instinct not to trust Lilith was justified although he had no proof the woman was deceitful. Still, he was in need of a distraction from Rosalinda and decided to continue playing along for a bit to see if his instincts proved correct. "And is your mother's assessment correct?" he asked, trying to keep the conversation flowing. "Are you enjoying yourself so far?"

She nodded.

"How fortunate to have friends to visit while you are here."

She stared at him a bit. "Excuse me?"

"You mentioned your mother was visiting friends this afternoon."

"Oh, yes. Of course." She gave a nervous laugh. "That was another reason mother chose Paris. They are old friends from New York."

Charles smiled. "Perhaps I have heard of them. What is their name?"

Aimée-Louise took a longer drink of water this time, as her eyes scanned the room. Setting the glass down once again, she said, "Bardot."

His eyes lit up. "Are they related to Brigitte?"

A frown formed on her lovely face. "Who?"

Chuckling, as he had a tough time believing this woman would not know who Brigitte Bardot was, he told her, "The actress. Brigitte Bardot. She was just nominated for a BAFTA Award."

Aimée-Louise's eyes widened. "I did not realize… has she been in any of your films?"

He mentally shook his head. If the woman was pretending, she wasn't very convincing, yet he couldn't deny his interest. There was something sad and lonely about her that drew him in. "I wouldn't object," he concluded, "to having her play a role if the right script presented itself."

"I will confess, I viewed the movie you made last year. Love in The Spring," She quoted the title. "It made me cry and laugh. Rosalinda Vallombrosa did an excellent job of portraying Lady Mary! I absolutely adore Rosalinda."

Charles sighed. He was trying not to think of Rosalinda, but she inserted herself into his thoughts, regardless of his wishes.

Why was Rosalinda always at the forefront of his thoughts? Why couldn't he fixate on her promiscuous behavior instead? Maybe if he could concentrate on that aspect of her character, he could start to despise her.

He simply could not bring himself to do it. He held too many precious memories of the quiet good she did, the kind of actions that often escaped the notice of everyone but him.

He had once witnessed her show kindness by comforting a homeless woman who sought shelter from the wind against a building. Then there was that warm summer day in the park: as he strolled to clear his mind, he had looked across the way to see her soothing a fallen child and assuring the child's anxious mother that all would be well.

He would never forget the ugly scene on the set of *Love in The Spring* when an actor with a bit part berated a young production assistant, a boy who supplied snacks and ran errands for the cast. The actor had cursed the poor boy and threatened his job, simply because the service hadn't been fast enough. Immediately, Rosalinda, like a general going to war, had marched right up to the man, who towered over her five-foot, five-inch frame, and put him firmly in his place.

But somehow, someway, Charles vowed to himself, he would stop obsessing over her. With that thought in mind, wanting to distract himself, he asked Aimée-Louise, "Would you and your mother like to have supper with me tonight?" He knew immediately how desperate he was to forget Rosalinda when he realized he had included Lilith in the invitation

Chapter Three

One Week Later

As Charles Lafayette finished his shower, the sound of voices from the television in his bedroom provided the usual background noise. But when he turned off the water, an advertisement for the play he planned to attend that evening caught his ear. He paused his routine, looking into the other room where the television screen was visible. The commercial was introducing the lead actress with her name and a photo, accompanied by a upbeat voice-over inviting people to the production tonight.

The photo was of Rosalinda.

It did not surprise him to see her image staring back at him. He knew she was the leading lady in this play.

He was taking a gamble tonight. If it failed, he would accept the loss and move on with his life. But since he had loved Rosalinda for so long, he knew he couldn't suddenly change his desires. He vowed to try a new strategy and hoped the decision wouldn't lead to regret.

It had killed him to watch her dancing with different men at her birthday party last month. He had barely gotten to tell her hello before another man had whisked her away onto the dance floor.

With a sigh, he glanced at his reflection in the bathroom mirror, pleased with the results of his efforts. He was glad he had paired weight-lifting with his diet. Where there was once flab, he now found a subtle washboard effect to his stomach, and the muscles in his arms were well-defined.

He scowled at his lacking head of hair and made a spur-of-the-moment decision to do something about it before he lost his nerve.

Rummaging through the vanity drawers, he found a pair of scissors and immediately began trimming the fringe of hair left on his head. He

knew he could have easily called his barber, who would have come over without hesitation. After all, Charles paid the man a hefty sum to tend to his thinning hair whenever he called.

Well, he would be out of a job, now, wouldn't he? Charles thought as he lathered up his scalp and took a fresh razor from the drawer.

He proceeded to shave off anything trying to remain behind. There would not be a need for a barber when a clean-shaven head was something he could take care of himself. Although keeping the man employed would not tax him financially.

After carefully shaving his scalp, Charles used his towel to wipe away any remaining residue. Gazing at his reflection, he was amazed by the transformation. While his face hadn't suddenly changed, the complete baldness seemed to have taken a few years off his appearance. And perhaps, without any distracting patches of hair, it had actually made him more attractive.

He speculated about what Rosalinda's reaction would be when she saw him.

Moving into the bedroom, he dressed for the evening.

Wearing one of his tailor-made gray suits, he proceeded into the grand hallway of the chateau's third-floor living space. This 24,000 square-foot 16th-century residence boasted thirteen rooms, including nine bedrooms and five bathrooms. Yet, for all the interior grandeur, his favorite place remained the gardens outside, centered around a magnificent swimming pool.

As he descended the staircase to the first floor, he could hear his mother speaking to someone in the living area and thought he recognized Aimée-Louise's voice.

He had invited her to attend the play with him this evening and would not feel guilt over the reason he had done so.

For the past week, he had used the dinner invitations as a way to figure out what their game was. He found that several things about them didn't quite add up, and he suspected they thought they could ensnare him into proposing marriage to Aimée-Louise.

He was not a gullible man. However, he enjoyed the distraction they provided. At least he had something else to occupy his mind while he tried to sort through the puzzle they seem to have created for him.

In truth, Charles liked Aimée-Louise, possibly as a friend, as they had common interests. The issue was her mother, who was clearly pushing her daughter toward him, and whom he genuinely disliked. He endured the woman's company only for Aimée-Louise, because the daughter sometimes seemed to fear her own mother and he wanted to know why that might be.

Tonight, however, Charles had asked only Aimée-Louise to attend the play with him.

Just a few days ago, Charles made the spur-of-the-moment decision to throw a party at his house this weekend. He had no particular reason to celebrate, but hoped a good gathering would boost his mood. His staff were already sending invitations to his list of close friends and handling all the necessary preparations.

He invited Aimée-Louise to the event, hoping she would meet others. He connected with her because he saw in her a loneliness that echoed his own. However, a mutual feeling of solitude was not a foundation for any kind of meaningful relationship.

Besides, fool that he was, his heart still belonged to Rosalinda.

The voices grew clearer in the foyer, confirming one was Aimée-Louise's. He frowned, recalling he was supposed to pick her up at her hotel, but the surprise was minimal: he still didn't know where she and her mother were staying. The women always skillfully evaded his inquiries by changing the subject, a secrecy that only intensified his suspicion.

Obviously, the women were determined to keep their lodging arrangements secret.

Pausing outside the living area, he glanced into the room. His mother looked frazzled, a state he could easily understand. He had observed at dinner several nights ago that when Aimée-Louise was nervous, she tended to talk a lot and listen little.

Stepping into the room, he said, "Aimée-Louise, I thought I mentioned I would pick you up at your hotel if you would have provide its location."

Patricia Lafayette, his mother, looked up with relief, then confusion crossed her face, as she noticed her son's appearance. "Charles, what happened to your hair?"

"Most of it left years ago, mother. What happened to the rest does not really matter, does it?"

She opened her mouth, then closed it, supposing he was right.

Aimée-Louise took in his appearance and gushed, "You look wonderful!" She glided the few feet toward him and proceeded quickly to kiss his cheeks in greeting.

"Thank you," he said, then asked again, "Why are you here?"

Again, she smiled brightly. "My mother wanted me to surprise you."

He shrugged, not knowing what to say to that. Her mother seemed to want to surprise him a lot.

Aimée-Louise glanced around the grandeur surrounding her. Something in her eyes reminded Charles of someone who always longed for something, but never acquired it.

After a moment, she looked at his mother and said softly, "You must be very proud of all he has accomplished."

Proud? Patricia knew no one could fully grasp her joy for the son she conceived at twenty-two years of age.

The pregnancy had been unwanted, a brutal consequence of a night when a gardener, employed at the estate where she worked as a maid, had cornered and raped her. When she discovered she was with child, the fear of losing her job was immediate. Frightened and knowing she couldn't possibly support both herself and a baby, she considered the unthinkable: leaving the infant on a nunnery's doorstep once it was born. No matter how desperately she tried to conceal the shame of being an unwed mother, she could not hide her growing belly.

Eventually, her employer, a seventy-year-old widower of nobility, had confronted her, asking about the child's father. Unable to lie, Patricia told the kind gentleman the truth.

The gardener disappeared the next day.

Her employer, guilt-ridden over the tragedy, proposed marriage. As he had no heirs, the arrangement was simple: his entire estate and wealth would be left to her and the unborn child upon his death.

Even after all these years, it still staggered her to have found true happiness, especially given her son's difficult beginnings. Despite the age difference, she had deeply loved Fernando Lafayette. He was a kind man who treated her son as though he were his own. They shared fifteen years together before Fernando passed away peacefully in his sleep at eighty-five, and Charles inherited the man's fortune, just as Fernando had promised.

Her true source of pride was what her son accomplished with the inherited wealth. He used it to attend college, graduated, and began a successful production company that made films. He was a gifted and caring man, a testament to the influence of his stepfather; one could easily believe Fernando had been his sire.

"Yes," Patricia said, "I am immensely proud of my son." She gave him an affectionate look and admitted to herself that he looked better without hair. He should have shaved it off long ago.

Drifting through the room, Aimée-Louise took in the furniture and artwork before stopping at the unlit fireplace. The mantle was lined with dozens of framed photos of Charles posing alongside celebrities from around the globe. She quickly noted that Rosalinda Vallombrosa appeared in a significant number of those pictures.

Aimée-Louise picked up the photo of Rosalinda and Charles. Though he was grinning but looking away, she immediately saw a flicker in the starlet's eyes, a look the camera had caught as Rosalinda fixed her gaze on him.

"She's in love with him," Aimée-Louise thought, realizing the irony; Charles would never be escorting someone else to Rosalinda's leading role performance if he knew she harbored feelings for him.

With a mental sigh, she acknowledged the choice she had to make and hoped it was the right one. For the first time in her life, she would defy her mother, help someone else, and damn the consequences.

Turning toward him, she told him, "Charles, is there some place we could talk? I have something to say.

Taken aback by the seriousness of her tone, he inclined his head. "This way," he said, and led her to his study and closed the door.

Chapter Four

Rosalinda stood on stage, basking in the thunderous applause.

Performing was not just a skill, but a spiritual necessity that fed her soul. Her gift was the ability to take words written by another and make them flow naturally from her lips, as though they were her own. This art of transformation, which entranced audiences and made a performance feel like a real-life event, was second nature to her and earned her the deep admiration of all France, including President Charles de Gaulle.

The curtain dropped, and the reverberating applause echoed off the walls, an experience that instantly made her feel most alive. Even with her heart feeling heavy that day, the chant of "Rosalinda, Rosalinda!" made it burst with joy.

She was a mere six-year-old child when the passion for the stage first hit. Taken by her mother to a local performance, she was mesmerized by the costumes and the audience's rapt attention. Observing the actors create an imaginary world on a simple plywood platform with two chairs, she made a sudden, definitive vow: she would be the best actress France had ever known.

Rosalinda certainly had competition. The sisters Françoise Dorléac and Catherine Deneuve already had several films to their credit. However, the true rival to beat was cinema actress Simone Signoret, who was already deeply embedded in the hearts of every French citizen. Despite the challenge, Rosalinda's own popularity was growing by leaps and bounds.

Clutching a bouquet of long-stemmed roses—a bold mix of cloud white and blood red—Rosalinda stood center stage as the curtain rose for the final bows. Her devoted fans, familiar with her taste, showered her with single-stem flowers, which landed on the dais at her feet. This nightly offering was their unique salute to her performance.

There were always too many delicate roses to keep. The small dressing room behind the stage could never hold so many. Better suited would have been her ten-room home on the outskirts of town, which included four bedrooms and three bathrooms. But those rooms would never know the pleasure of having the fragrance of these roses permeate their walls.

She never kept the roses. Instead of hoarding the nightly tokens of affection, Rosalinda preferred to share her appreciation by distributing the flowers throughout the city. Her staff was tasked with delivering the bouquets to hospitals, bringing a bit of color to the otherwise bleak rooms of the sick. The remaining flowers were sent by her secretary to nursing homes, where residents' faces would light up whenever the fresh arrangements appeared in the visitor's section.

The regifting of flowers was a secret. No one who received them knew where the fragrant donation came from. But they speculated to themselves, and others, that possibly Rosalinda Vallombrosa had sent them. It was common knowledge that she liked to give roses to those who were sick or forgotten.

On stage now, she blew kisses with her right hand to the audience. Then, as she turned to go backstage, her eye caught sight of a man sitting in the front row.

She almost stumbled.

The man was in a stunning gray suit, and his head appeared to be glistening in the hall lights. He was familiarly handsome, which drew Rosalinda's attention. As she slowly turned to look at the man again, she could feel her heart beginning to race, as she realized the beautiful man seated before her was… Charles?!

From where she stood, she could almost swear his head was bald, gone were the tuffs of hair she knew so well, and oh-my-god, what a difference it made in his appearance. Combined with his previous weight loss, he seemed extraordinarily handsome tonight. For the first time since she had known him, she felt a powerful desire for him arise from deep within her.

The magnetic pull to him had been ever increasing, and she did not think she could fight it any longer. Perhaps it was time. Maybe she was

ready. Perhaps, she had finally matured enough to understand that what she had always craved was right there in front of her.

She knew that with him, it would never be a one-night stand. With him, she knew there would be commitment.

He was of average height; close to five feet seven with shoes on, but next to her five foot five inches, he was tall enough.

An aura of command surrounded him, but she knew he wasn't a cruel man. Their three months together in Cannes, filming the movie that launched them both to global stardom, proved it. While he could bark out orders to efficiently get the job done, he always maintained respect, never belittling his crew.

Taking on both director and producer roles for his latest film, Charles insisted on rigorous rehearsals. He was uncompromising; if an angle was off or a line delivery missed his vision, he had them start over from the beginning. Still, the cast and crew rarely complained, especially as the film took shape. They knew Charles Lafayette was a fair man, and working on his production meant you were working for the best in the business.

Those who worked for him loved him, and with certainty, she knew he loved her.

She knew, deep in her heart, that this was true. Over the twelve years she'd known him, Charles had consistently shown her respect and honor, even when she didn't deserve it. He never once suggested anything lewd or asked her to join him in his bed—a complete contrast to her own past. She, after all, used to take lovers purely for pleasure whenever she fancied a conquest.

But she hadn't sought a conquest in a long, long time.

Knowing Charles did not view her as a sex object staggered her and brought forth a sea of emotional waves. Her feelings for him had always been at odds with her stronger and wild nature. But something had changed in her, and she acknowledged it was time for her to stop fighting his allure.

She wondered how she could possibly tell him he was, indeed, her very heart. After all this time, would he think she played games with his emotions?

Knowing she needed to move off the stage, she forced her eyes away from Charles, but as she did, she took notice of the person sitting next to him. It was a woman, one who had her arms draped around him, no less.

The hussy appeared to be whispering secrets in his ear.

Unknowingly, Rosalinda's eyes narrowed to slits.

Was that woman caressing his cheek?!

The very idea of Charles on a date was hard to fathom. He had never once, in all their twelve years of acquaintance, appeared in public with a woman. While rumors persisted that he preferred men, Rosalinda dismissed the gossip instantly. She had seen the fire in his eyes when he glanced at her—a clear, male desire that men who preferred men simply did not possess.

The curtain dropped, cutting off her view of the couple.

She stood on the stage, behind the curtain, staring at the thick cloth, while stagehands scurried around her. It felt as though she were in shock. And she felt a blinding urge to march down the steps, leading from the stage to the audience, and pull every strand of hair out from the woman's head.

Why on earth was Charles with that woman?

The answer was clear, and Rosalinda felt tears surfacing. He had obviously decided to forget about her.

"Rosalinda!" She felt a hand on her elbow and turned to see Walter, her stage manager, standing next to her. "What is wrong with you? You need to get off the stage."

What she wanted to do was march down the steps and sock the woman in the nose.

Walter tugged on her arm. "Rosalinda, did you hear me?"

She took a deep breath. She knew she had work to do, but it had nothing to do with the play. But there was nothing she could do about it now.

"I heard you, Walter." She muttered as she allowed him to lead her toward her dressing room.

As usual, Walter had to fight off her fans waiting backstage, wanting an autograph or just a touch from her.

It always amazed her, the boldness of people. Someone could be their next-door neighbor and never acknowledge their existence. But, let that same person become an international celebrity, and suddenly, they treat the person as though they were a god.

But she knew this was part of her fame. So, she signed the pieces of paper extended her way from hopeful fans and shook hands with others. Even now, as her heart was breaking, she forced herself to smile and laugh gaily as Walter continued to push and shove through the crowd. Finally, pulling her behind him, moving toward the door of the room reserved for the star of the show, they broke free from the masses.

Upon reaching the room, Walter opened the door, then pressed in behind her, just managing to close and lock the entrance as the crowd continued trying to press in.

"Rosalinda," Walter gasped, worn out from fighting his way through the throng. "Honestly, you need to reconsider another means of getting from the stage to here."

She turned toward him; a smile developed on her lips as she were about to say something. But whatever Rosalinda would have said stopped in her throat upon seeing the man standing in front of the locked door. "Dominic!" she exclaimed and leaped into the man's open arms. Her shock of seeing Charles with another woman; momentarily forgotten.

Walter placed a hand on his heart, as though he were about to have a heart attack. "Damn it all to hell, Dominic! You scared ten years off my life, which I cannot afford to lose."

Rosalinda's youngest brother sent him an unrepented grin over the top of his sister's head, though he begged forgiveness. "Forgive me, Walter," he laughed. "Honestly, I was not hiding. I came in seconds ago and was just behind the door when it opened. It is not my fault you did not see me right away."

Rosalinda rolled her eyes. "Most people would continue walking into the room; not stand behind the door once it is closed." She gave him a quick sisterly kiss on his cheek, which, given his height, was not an easy thing for her to do. Whenever she was around her brothers, she always felt as though she were the runt of the litter. All four of them were six feet tall and towered over her.

Stepping away from him, she moved to the small vanity. Sitting down on the low-backed chair, she reached into the cobalt glass bottle of Pond's Cream. Touching the cream to her face, she began smearing it over her forehead, nose, and jaw to aid in the removal of the heavily caked stage make-up. Then, with a face full of goo, she turned back to her brother and smiled through the mask of white. "We were not expecting you home until next week."

Dominic moved farther into the room, shrugged carelessly. "I finished my business in New York City earlier than expected and took a trip out west." Reaching out, he ran a finger down his sister's face, leaving a trail mark in the facial cream. "Jacqueline asked me to give you a kiss on the cheek. I will not do it because it is covered up with that goop, but I will tell you hello from her. She is looking forward to your visit in a few weeks."

He smiled. "I knew she was expecting again, but I had not thought she would look so pregnant when I saw her."

Rosalinda laughed; her eyes sparkled. "Dear brother, she does not have much time left before the baby's due date. Did you really believe she would still be thin?"

"This play ends soon," Rosalinda continued, wiping the facial cream off, as she faced the mirror once more. "When it does, I will travel to North Dakota. I am eager to spend time with Clinton and Donna." She adored Jacqueline's three-year-old daughter and ten-year-old stepson.

Dominic suddenly changed the conversation and asked, "Have you hired a bodyguard?"

Walter rolled his eyes and grumbled, "She says she does not need one."

Dominic's frown held displeasure.

Rosalinda threw her hands in the air as though by doing so, she could rid herself of this conversation. "Walter does a wonderful job of keeping people away from me when he escorts me to my dressing room."

"Oh, yes. Such an outstanding job," Walter said, raising his left arm and showing them his torn sleeve. "I do not like having to replace my shirts every day."

She laughed.

Walter glowered at the raven-haired goddess. "You need a real body-guard. Why do you keep putting it off?"

Rosalinda shrugged. She would not discuss her reluctance with either of them.

Walter knew she could be stubborn and kept his mouth shut. They had this conversation countless times over the past three years. She had a bodyguard at one time; however, he had died. Walter did not know the details, but Rosalinda seemed unwilling to hire anyone else to replace the vacant position.

Dominic, on-the-other-hand, knowing his sister's pigheadedness better than anyone said, "You will have one by tomorrow morning. Father is, at this moment, interviewing for the position."

Rosalinda gasped. "Dominic…!"

"Tomorrow," he snapped it out like a bullet leaving a gun. Rosalinda's body involuntarily jerked at the explosion. "We worry for you! You know that. You have been fortunate these past years not to have some-one follow you home or confront you in public. But since you do not seem capable of finding one on your own, you have forced our hand."

"Dominic!" she exclaimed again and felt as though she were a child, not a grown woman.

He held up his hand to stop her. "Enough, Rose. It will be done."

She would not win this argument, no matter how much she protested.

Dominic did not raise his voice often. Not to her, at least. Obviously, her lack of a guard bothered her family more than she would have guessed.

Not wanting to argue, she let the matter go. "Sometimes, you are a bore, brother."

He leaned down and kissed her on her now clean face. "A bore who loves you," he told her gently.

Her throat tightened with emotion. She knew how fortunate she was to have a close-knit family who loved and supported her.

Walter cleared his throat, uncomfortable with the siblings show of affection. "Your performance tonight was exceptional," he told Rosalinda. "There were moments I became lost in the show and forgot it was not real. I wept tonight when you killed your lover."

Rosalinda placed the lid back onto the Ponds container and smiled knowingly at her older friend. "You cry every night, Walter. Everyone knows you are in love with Andy." Andy being the thirty-five-year-old, and extremely handsome, actor who played the leading man in this production. Who wouldn't be infatuated with him? "You," she continued, "loathe the thought of anything really happening to him."

Walter's blush covered his entire face.

Chuckling, Rosalinda moved from the vanity and stepped behind a cream-colored, gold-trimmed dressing screen set in the corner of the room to change.

"I am not in love with Andy," Walter denied with a huff.

Dominic rolled his eyes. He knew which way the wind blew with Walter, having had the man make advances toward him a while back. Dominic believed everyone had the right to love who they chose. But, since he preferred women, he had told Walter to keep his hands to himself.

Rosalinda peeked out from behind the screen. "Yes, you are, and you are afraid Tommy will find out about it."

This time Walter could not dispute her words. His partner, Tommy, was a jealous man. If he knew Walter was looking at another man, there would be hell to pay. Not that Tom was abusive. It wasn't like that. But when Tom became angry, he liked to throw things. And Wal-ter did not like the mess it created for him.

A knock on the door had the three of them looking in that direction. One never knew who might be behind the closed door.

Sometimes a fan would be bold enough to loiter in the outer hall, waiting for others to leave before finding the courage to knock on Rosalinda's door to ask for an autograph or to propose. She had had plenty of men throughout her career, ask her to marry them.

It amazed her, though it shouldn't, that a man, and a few women, proclaimed their love based on who they thought she was. They created their own fantasy about her based on what they read in a magazine, or through a performance she had given.

Rosalinda stepped out from behind the screen, dressed in an elegant Tailleur suit, the color of a moonbeam; its collar trimmed with mink.

Walter moved to the door. "Mademoiselle Vallombrosa is not signing autographs!" he called out, assuming the person on the other side of the door was there to gain a signature from the actress, so they could later brag to family and friends that they had met the famous Rosalinda.

The person knocked a second time. "It is Charles Lafayette," came the rich baritone in reply.

Walter's eyes snapped to Rosalinda's in silent question.

Rosalinda stared at the door, her heart drumming in her ears. For a moment, she had forgotten the heartache of seeing him tonight. But she would not be a coward. At her nod, Walter cautiously opened the door.

Into the room rushed a blur of red silk that almost knocked Walter down. Rosalinda's eyes widened as she braced for impact; the woman was heading straight toward her.

Aimée-Louise Fontaine reached Rosalinda in four quick strides. She put her arms around her, delivering a tight squeeze. "Darling!" she purred in French, her American accent thick.

Rosalinda's eyes immediately locked onto Charles as he walked through the doorway, trailing the woman she saw as a beast wrapped in silk. At that precise moment, Aimée-Louise's lips brushed hers in a quick, forced peck of affection that only made Rosalinda's stomach lurch.

Rosalinda struggled to free herself from the unwanted embrace. A glance at her brother told her the display had amused Dominic.

"Darling," Aimée-Louise repeated, releasing her hold. "Your performance tonight was exceptional! You had me on the edge of my seat."

"Thank you," Rosalinda managed to say, stepping out of reach, and hoped the woman wouldn't follow. If she did, Rosalinda knew she would go through with her desire to sock her in the nose.

Breezing on as though she hadn't a care in the world, Aimée-Louise told her, "I am happy Charles insisted I attend your little play with him tonight." Now she moved to Charles' side, kissed him on the cheek. "Thank you, darling."

Rosalinda's jaw ached as her teeth ground together. The rush of jealousy she experienced almost knocked her off her feet. To see Aimée-Louise wrapped around Charles as though staking a claim had her lips thinning, hackles rising. What in the name of God was Charles doing with that dimwit?

Charles wrapped an arm around Aimée-Louise's trim waist, pulled her snug against him. "I would not have had it any other way," he insisted, smiling at the blond as though she were the only woman in the room that mattered.

It made Rosalinda's skin crawl.

Aimée-Louise beamed as though he had given her a 14k diamond ring.

Charles turned his attention to Dominic without looking again at Rosalinda. "It is good to see you, my friend."

Dominic shook his hand, laughter dancing behind his eyes due to the spectacle transpiring before him. "You look well."

Charles had been a few years ahead of Dominic in college, in his study of everything concerning filmmaking; Dominic had been earnestly studying women when he wasn't in the classroom. Back then, Dominic had chosen a career in accounting and finance. The problem with that was the teachers could not show him anything he had not already known. He had grown bored, dropped out, and followed his heart, his passion.

Rosalinda's brother was a talented artist and illustrator. His recent trip to the United States had allowed him the opportunity to show his work in one of New York City's famous galleries. It had been a successful showing. Several people commissioned him to paint portraits of their loved ones. There was enough work lined up to keep him busy for a year and a half.

"I like the new look," Dominic referred to Charles' now shaved head.

Charles smiled, touched the clean scalp. "I decided if my friend Yul Brynner was bold enough to shave his head when he starred in the King and I, it could not hurt if I did the same."

Turning to Rosalinda, Charles told her, "As always, your performance was flawless. I am hosting a party at my chateau Saturday night and would like to invite you personally," he glanced at Dominic, "Both of you, of course."

Dominic looked between Charles, Aimée-Louise, and his sister. "I would not miss it for the world." The amusement in his eyes seemed to grow, as though he knew a showdown was brewing.

"Excellent," Charles smiled back at him. It was more of a grin, as if to agree with Dominic's assumption.

"Rose?" Dominic turned his attention to his sister, who seemed to have developed daggers in her eyes, and was mentally tossing them at Aimée-Louise. He could not help his pleasure at seeing Rosalinda, finally in an emotional state over Charles. Dominic had always believed Charles was the perfect match for his only sister. "Would you like to attend the party with me?"

It took a moment for her to respond. She did not like Charles being with some, some... Well, she did not know what this Aimée-Louise was, but she certainly wasn't good enough for Charles.

"Of course, I would love to attend your gathering," she told Charles, her heart drumming as she met those copper-colored eyes of his. Obviously, someone needed to protect him from untrustworthy females.

Charles' grin reminded Dominic of a Cheshire cat. "Wonderful!" Taking Aimée-Louise's hand in his he told her, "Come along, dear."

As they walked out the door, they heard him say, "I believe I shall take you for lunch tomorrow. I am certain you will enjoy dining at La Tour d'Argent."

Chapter Five

Half-way across the world.

In the early morning hours south of Medora, North Dakota, Cadman Benson rode like the city slicker he was. Stiff as a board, he bounced uncomfortably in the saddle as his horse trotted along the dusty trail. The sun seemed to conspire in his torment: even at this hour, its heat bore down unmercifully, baking the already hardened ground and sucking every last bit of moisture from the earth left over from the harsh winter.

He bit off a groan when he saw the rider ahead of him glance back and cursed instead. "For the love of God, Colt! Couldn't we just walk 'em instead?"

Colten Fisher reined in his horse, a chuckle escaping him. "For the sake of your horse, I think that's a good idea," he said. "You'll break its back if you don't learn to relax and go with it, instead of against it." As their mounts slowed to a walk, Colten maneuvered to Cadman's left side. This position allowed him to keep his friend easily in view, a necessity since his left eye was destroyed three years ago protecting the woman who was now his wife from a madman.

"I don't know how you always manage to talk me into coming out here." Cadman griped, breathing a silent sigh of relief, now that the horse he was on wasn't trying to launch him into outer space.

Colten's smile was full of boyish innocence. "You like it here. You're just too stubborn to admit it."

Cadman's gaze swept over the desolate and arid terrain known as the Badlands. The name was fitting for the rugged landscape surrounding them - canyons, towering spires, flat-topped mesas, and vast grassy plains dominated this area. Despite its roughness, there was still something alluring about this place. Cadman couldn't deny that fact, even though he despised horses—he loathed them with a fiery passion. "I

only come out here to ensure that the woman I love is being well looked after," he stated firmly.

Colten grinned and then laughed, "You saw her swollen belly. Proof enough, she's been taken care of properly." Colten was head-over-heels in love with his wife, who they were currently discussing.

Cadman sighed. "She keeps telling me she's happy with you." He shook his head, as though the very idea gave him indigestion. Truthfully, though, it pleased him to know the two of them were still as committed to each other today as they had been when they had taken their vows.

Colten pointed to a fence line; nudged his horse in that direction.

Cadman groaned, seeing the downed wire. He would have sworn they'd already fixed every line of barbed wire between here and Dickinson, the closest community of sizable numbers from their location. And that was at least thirty-eight miles east of where they were now.

Colten laughed at hearing his friend's sound of despair.

Although Cadman was only five years older than Colten, who was now thirty-three, he couldn't help but tease the guy. "Come on, old man. We'll finish this one, then head on back for some coffee and a break."

At the thought of coffee, Cadman almost sighed dreamily. A break from mending fences, and the damn horse, had him wanting to weep with joy. "Don't tease me," he grumbled, stepping down from the beast of torment.

Colten slipped on his work gloves, picked up the downed wire, and frowned at the broken section. "Hand me one of those short pieces of wire in my saddlebag," he instructed, as he prepared the broken segment for the splice he would add before stretching the section.

Handing the two-foot-long barbed wire to the ex-Secret Service agent, Cadman shook his head. "You actually like doing this stuff," he marveled.

Grinning, Colten nodded as he looped the ends of the broken section together with the new wire. "It's a hell of a lot safer than what you do," he claimed, going to work with a hammer pulling the wire tight.

With a shrug, Cadman reached for the canteen of water hanging from the saddle horn of the horse Colten had forced him to ride on this mission of checking for a downed wire.

"There's been talk about making up a new task force," Cadman said softly as he watched Colten work.

The information was top secret. The upper brass would hang his balls out to dry if they knew he had told anyone about it. But this was Colten: an honorable man who wouldn't gossip. Someone who had stood with him several times before his chosen retirement.

"Yeah?" was all Colten said, as he removed his hat to wipe the sweat from his forehead.

Cadman nodded. "The idea is still in its preliminary stages. People would be hand-picked from every area of government. Army, Marines…." he waved a hand. "Top notch elite force."

The brow over Colten's good eye rose half an inch. "You're telling me this because you're still pissed that I retired, and hoping I'll be locked up or killed if the government found out I know about this?" He said it with a straight face, but there was humor around the edges of his eye.

Cadman blew out a breath. "No, I'm telling you because they are looking at me to head it up."

For one moment, Colten stared at his friend as though he'd grown two heads, then broke into a round of laughter. "Good God, you sound as though it's a curse rather than an honor."

"Maybe it's both. I don't know what my answer is. I have a few months to think about it."

Colten slapped him on the back, a congratulate, hang-in-there-partner, manly gesture. "If that's your way of asking me for advice, I can tell you they couldn't have chosen anyone better. You're an asset to them, and they know it. You have run the special branch of Secret Service, which blends with other government sectors, better than anyone could have. It's about time they promote you to something that would be lucky to have your talent for organization, and combat skills."

The sudden lump in his throat caused Benson to cough and take another swig of water to wash it down. He had not known he'd been fishing for approval from this man until he had it. "Did you say some-thing about coffee?" he asked once he found his voice; changing the subject smoothly, regardless of the fact they both knew embarrassment had him doing so.

They mounted up and rode in silence. Colten, being retired from the government, had enough memories of what men could do to others that would last him a lifetime. He was not sorry he no longer served. But he was glad to know men like Cadman dedicated their lives to tracking the bad guys, keeping America as safe as humanly possible.

Cresting the top of a butte, Colten spotted a rider coming their way at breakneck speed. For a moment, he became concerned that a tourist, who had come for an adventure into the badlands, was getting more than he had bargained for. But when he recognized the mount, he knew who the rider was, and his tension eased; it was Clinton.

Doctors diagnosed his eldest child with autism a long time ago. People considered Clinton high functioning in his disability. Someone who met him for the first time would never suspect. But the boy had a few quirks that set him apart from others. A person might notice his obsessing over certain things if they were around him long enough. But Clinton excelled in horsemanship.

Colten's heart swelled with pride as he watched his son gather the horse for a jump. It flew over the fallen logs in its path, as though it had sprouted wings. Horse and rider landed on the other side with ease and grace. Then continued at the fast gallop, as though they had not just jumped an area a more experienced horseman might have considered going around.

Cadman whistled. "Ya think I could hire Clinton to teach me how to ride like that?"

"Cadman, you can hardly sit on a horse as it is." Colten pointed out, earning him a glare from the other man.

"He looks upset," Cadman said, as the ten-year-old continued closing the distance.

Colten squinted; felt his heart leap to his throat. Clinton absolutely looked troubled. His first thought was that something had happened to Jacqueline or their daughter. Apprehension had him urging his own mount into action. Leaving Cadman at the top of the butte he headed at a fast pace toward his eldest son.

"Dad, dad, dad!" Clinton shouted, raining in when the two horses met up at the bottom of the bluff.

"What happened? Who's hurt?" Colten asked, his voice coming out sharp with concern.

Clinton looked confused at his father's anxious questions.

Colten grabbed his arm. "Son. Focus! Is something wrong with mom?"

The boy's face scrunched up. "I don't think so. Should there be?"

Colten took a deep breath and counted to ten. Moments like this always made the old resentment rear its head. He had once struggled to accept his son's autism, but he'd since moved past it, learning to see the wonderful child beneath the peculiarities. Yet, sometimes, that familiar, ugly tide of impatience still rushed back in.

Cadman's horse came up alongside father and son. The man was proud of the fact he had made it down the hill without falling off the sixteen-hand sorrel quarter horse he had been riding all morning. Going down that incline had been harder than going up. It had felt as though he would slide right over the horse's head. As casually as he could, considering his heart was thumping from his unease of maneuvering the mount, without Colten beside him, he asked Clinton, "Hey, buddy. What's up?"

"Mom said I had to get you. Important phone call from Washington." Clinton beamed with the fact he had remembered what his mother had told him.

"Me?" Cadman clarified. "I'm on vacation."

Colten raised a brow. "Well, if that don't beat all. I clearly remember a vacation I had coming to me a few years ago, and both you and the President denied it"

Cadman beamed a grin at him. "Well, hell, Colten. You managed to get yourself a beautiful wife out of the deal."

"Well, gosh, maybe there's hope for you yet. And who knows, this vacation will lead to your own blissful marriage."

Cadman visibly shuddered with the thought. He had no plans of marriage in the near future. He preferred bachelorhood.

Clinton reached out, intent on taking the reins from Cadman if the man did not come immediately. His mother had said it was important for Uncle Cadman to come quickly. To Clinton, this meant right now!

Colten reached out his own hand to stop the boy. "He can manage on his own," he told his son, seeing the intent on the kids' face.

"Mom said he had to come fast!"

Colten's brow arched skyward as he glanced at Cadman and drawled, "You hear that, Cadman? Time to fly like the wind."

Cadman shook his head. "Not in this lifetime." He set the horse into a leisurely walk. "I'll get there soon enough." In one piece, he thought to himself.

It took a good forty-five minutes to reach Colten's ranch at their slow pace. But Cadman did not mind the long ride since he had not bounced once in the saddle.

Cresting the final butte, he marveled at the property's transformation. The Fisher's magnificent home now dominated a rise where only thorn bushes had once grown, with the entire ranch spread out below. The busy stables stretched out beneath the house, where employees prepared horses for waiting tourists. Visitors could choose between a thirty-minute or an hour-long guided tour, the length dictated by the price they were willing to pay. Both rides allowed them to experience the Badlands' beauty from unbeatable vantage points.

The newly constructed mess hall provided three square meals daily for all: tourists and the Fisher staff. Most of the ranch hands were seasonal, hired just for the summer, and only a handful remained for the cold, secluded winter months. Among the permanent residents was Juan López, a twenty-year-old ex-pickpocket from New York who took great pride in running the hall. His small house sat behind the mess hall and was currently being expanded to make room for his bride, as the couple, married earlier this year, planned to start a family.

The Fisher's added something new each year to enhance one's visit. And each year, more people came for an experience of a lifetime.

The horses stopped before the enormous home, a structure grand enough for the hills of Beverly Hills, yet somehow perfectly integrated into the rugged landscape.

Once Benson and Colten dismounted, Clinton led the horses back down the incline where he would see to their needs. The boy knew horses like the back of his hand. It was the main thing he obsessed over, other than being ever watchful for his three-year-old sister. He took his role as big brother seriously. Which was a good thing; Donna could be a handful sometimes.

Jacqueline came out the door, her waist-length dark blond hair pulled back in a ponytail. "Cadman," she said, her swollen belly preceding her as she rushed toward them. Cadman had to grin. The woman did not let pregnancy slow her down. "You had a phone call from Washington."

"So, I heard," he glanced at Clinton's retreating form. "He was quite insistent that I come back here, at your request."

Colten put his arm around his wife, pulling her against his side. Something was wrong. It was clear on her face. She was as white as a sheet.

"The call was from your office." She waved a hand toward the house. "You're to call immediately, and they left a message…" Her eyes, filled with terror, locked with Colten's as she said, "Pierre escaped from Flury Mérogis prison."

Colten's arms tightened around his wife.

"What!?" Cadman's single question was a sonic boom. "That's not possible! I was just there last month!" Without another word, he marched into the house to call his agency. This was a nightmare of magnitude proportions.

Jacqueline burrowed her face into her husband's neck and held him tightly.

"He won't come here," Colten promised. "He thinks we're dead."

"I know that," she sniffed. Raising her face to his, she said, "But Rosalinda is in Paris."

Colten wasn't sure he had anything to say that would comfort her. His wife's concern for her best friend was real. Rosalinda possibly was a target for Pierre, as she had helped Jacqueline to escape from him three years ago. "Let's go inside," he said insisted, as he opened the front door for her. Clinton and the hired help would see to the needs of the tourists. They had needs of their own right now.

They found Cadman sitting at Colten's desk, where their housekeeper, Sara, had directed him for the private call. There wouldn't be any secrets between him and the Fishers. Jacqueline needed to know what steps Cadman would take to ensure Rosalinda's safety.

Cadman slammed the receiver down, ending the call. "Damn it!" he exploded, immediately closing his eyes and pinching the bridge of his nose to force himself to calm down.

Colten stepped forward. "What happened? How did he get out?"

Cadman shook his head. "No one seems to know exactly how he managed to walk out the door. But a guard was found dead and stripped of his uniform."

"Rosalinda?" Jacqueline whispered.

"Since no one had reason to connect her to him, she hasn't been informed she might be in danger. I've instructed my office to contact the French authorities to send someone to protect her immediately."

The baby Jacqueline carried gave a kick so strong, it had her almost doubling over as she gasped out a startled breath. It felt as though the child wanted to break out and go after the fugitive itself.

He rushed to her side, circled her with his arms, and carefully guided her into a nearby chair. "Do we need the hospital?" he demanded. In moments like this, he bitterly regretted that the nearest medical facility was a good thirty minutes away.

She shook her head, rubbing her belly. "No, I'm fine," she assured him, instantly understanding his fear. He had lost his first wife while delivering Clinton, and the thought of losing her in the same way weighed heavily on him. Reaching up, she stroked his cheek. "I'm fine," she repeated, "it's just that ever since I heard Pierre was free, the baby has

been doing a kick dance. I think my anxiety is affecting its mood." She attempted a reassuring smile, but it faltered.

"Maybe you should lie down…," he began. The look Jacqueline sent him stopped the suggestion cold. His wife was healthy. Strong. He needed to remember that. He cleared his throat. "Have I told you to-day that I love you?"

She smiled at him. "I never get tired of you telling me."

Cadman walked around the desk, heading for the door. "I've got to pack and catch a plane. I'm heading to France." He stopped by Jacqueline, squeezing her shoulder. "You're sure you're all right?"

"Yes." Her answer was a mix of frustration and laughter. The baby had stopped its kicking, and she was feeling better for it. "Keep Rosalinda safe, Cadman."

With his heart hammering with fear for his sometimes lover, he nodded and continued on his way to his room to pack for the trip overseas. A thousand questions ran through his mind. The prison was maximum security. No way in hell could Pierre have walked out that door without help.

Sick with dread but trusting the French authorities to send someone to guard Rosalinda, Cadman all but ran through the house to reach his bedroom. He hated the fact he would have to drive forty-five miles to the nearest airport, then find a flight that would give him the proper connections to Paris.

Chapter Six

Delays in flights prevented Cadman from boarding the last plane bound for Paris until four in the morning. While he was buckling into his seat, impatient for the flight to reach its destination, Rosalinda's maid was waking the starlet up.

It was ten in the morning in France.

Rosalinda's maid informed her that her father and brothers were at the door, insisting on a meeting. Already in a foul mood from the early hour, she exploded into a temper upon learning they had brought a man, hired at daybreak, to serve as her bodyguard. Pacing furiously in her living room, she repeated, for what felt like the hundredth time, "I do not believe it!" Her animated gestures betrayed her French, Spanish, and Italian heritage.

"You understand this is because we love you?" her father said. "We have given you enough time to find a suitable guard, but you have not. Therefore, we retained one for you."

"I do not believe it!" This time when she said it, she rushed her hands through her raven black mane of hair in annoyance.

Her oldest brother, Theodore, rolled his eyes. "Do you not know how to say anything else, Rose?" He had said the family's nickname for her with affection, though his own exasperation was in the tone.

Dominic sat behind his sister's Marquetry inlaid French Louis XV writing desk. He leaned back in the chair, lifted his legs, and stretched them out on top of it. Lighting a cigarette, he admired the high sheen polished layers of varnish. He knew, without doubt, the piece of furniture was as expensive as hell.

He glanced at Rosalinda's scowling face and grinned, enjoying this performance perhaps a little more than he should.

Rosalinda glanced at the one man in the room not related to her and admitted he was as attractive as sin. Yet, for the first time, she felt no inclination to take him to bed. Rosalinda liked handsome men and

viewed sex as a healthy exercise, but her libido had been absent for months. Now, the only person she craved was the one who kept haunting her dreams, a man whose mere thought was enough to awaken her deepest longings.

Leopold and Frederic, the brothers who had been born between Theodore and Dominic, leaned casually against the fireplace. They weren't much for words, but they supported their father's decision to employ the bodyguard. They would protect their sister with their very lives if ever there was a need. But, unless their wives were willing to have her move in with them, which was not an option, they wanted to know she had someone with her around the clock. For now, they were keeping a low profile and not uttering a word. As much as they agreed with everything their father and oldest brother were saying, they did not intend to draw their sister's attention to themselves.

An upset Rosalinda was not pleasant.

With a deep sigh, Rosalinda turned toward the unwelcome man. She supposed it was poor manners to discuss him while he was present, but there was no help for it.

"Randolph," she began, addressing the hired man.

"Rudolph," he corrected. "Rudolph Forshaw."

A throbbing headache began as she rubbed her temples. She hadn't asked for this; she absolutely did not want another person who might die on her account. Three years later, Ralph's death still invaded her sleep. The memory was indelible: the bullet hitting his forehead, his body crumpling right next to her, and his lifeless eyes staring as if he couldn't fathom what had just happened.

"Rudolph," she amended. "Please, I do not mean to offend."

He offered a brilliant smile, one Rosalinda should have found sensual, yet she felt nothing but a cool appreciation for his perfectly straight, white teeth. "Mademoiselle," he said with a slight bow. "I am very good at my job, and I assure you, I would die if need be to protect you."

She cried out, ran from the room, stricken by the very thought.

On a sigh, Dominic removed his legs from the desk and said, "Merde." He stood up, looked around the room at his brothers, and told them, "Try not to kill him while I am gone." With that, he left the room in search of his sister to comfort and console. The stupid man had said the one thing that would almost guarantee Rosalinda would refuse his employment with her. But, by God, Dominic vowed, she would see reason and understand dismissing the bodyguard was not an option.

"Imbecile," Theodore hissed at Rudolph. It didn't matter that the man couldn't have known his declaration was the absolute worst thing to say. Now, Rosalinda would likely fight the hiring tooth and nail, making an already difficult situation unbearable for the family.

As his brothers and father berated Rudolph, Dominic took a moment to absorb the elegant living room. Its light cream furniture, accented with touches of green, perfectly complemented the oil painting above the cream-colored fireplace. The room itself was a seamless blend of casual comfort and elegance, mirroring his sister's personality, which explained why she was so adored. Rosalinda never flaunted the wealth and stature that came with being a Vallombrosa. In this, she favored their great-uncle Amédée: just as he refused his noble titles to be known only for his music, Rosalinda wanted to be remembered solely for her ability as an actress.

Dominic found her in her garden, sitting on a bench. Behind her, a waterfall statue of Aphrodite, surrounded by roses and gladiolus, looked down at her. He should have known the Goddess of Love and Beauty would be his sister's favorite deity. Both she and the Goddess had been with many lovers. He knew the lifestyle his sister lived and would not judge her for it. He wasn't a saint himself.

Seeing her cry made him feel sick to his stomach. He never really knew what to do with an emotional woman. He could not trust a female to react in a good way when a man was trying to console. Sometimes women attacked the comforter and accused them of not under-standing a woman's needs and emotions.

No joke. If Dominic understood women, he might have married by now. But he did not understand the emotional things and was not about to tie himself to one.

Taking a deep breath for courage, he sat down next to her and remained silent, hoping for inspiration.

Her sobs tore at his heart.

He almost told her to stop crying but held his tongue. She probably needed to grieve for the man who had sacrificed his life to protect her. So, he sat and waited until her sobs faded before reaching out his arm, pulling her against him, and allowing the remaining tears to fall onto his chest.

As she quieted, the only sounds they heard were the babbling of the water cascading from the container in Aphrodite's hands, into the pool at her feet. A few birds chirped to each other and were probably asking one an-other, "what do you think the humans will do next?"

"Rose," he said gently, "You know we want you to be as safe as you can be. Why does this affect you so?"

He felt her shrug; rested his chin on top of her head.

"Father, Mother, Theodore, Leopold, Frederic, and I need peace of mind, Rose. Ralph's death was not your fault...." He regretted the immediate sniffle his words provoked, realizing he'd opened the floodgates again. Ignoring his mistake, he continued firmly: "His death was not your fault. Everyone in protection knows the risks. Blame Pierre Bellefeuille, Rose. It was his bullet that put Ralph in the ground, not you. Your guilt makes you believe you could have controlled the situation." He kissed the top of her head. "Life, my dear sister, is full of twists and turns. We never know what's around the bend, and we certainly don't control it."

She looked up at him. Those cat-green eyes she had inherited from their mother, full of sorrow. But she gave him a shaky smile. "When did you become so smart?" Her voice sounded raw with emotion, but at least she was no longer crying.

"I have always been a genius, but you have been too stubborn to admit it."

His statement managed to get a slight smile out of her.

"Something else is bothering you, Rose? What is it?"

He had always been sensitive to her emotions. Even when they were children, he would know, without her saying anything, when she was feeling down.

"It is nothing."

"Which means it is something. You might as well tell me. I will pry it from you one way or the other."

True enough, Dominic had that skill too. "I am concerned for Charles Lafayette."

Dominic almost choked on a laugh as he attempted to cut it off. He had watched her last night, glaring at the Fontaine woman. Had she finally realized she loved the man? For years he had watched her deny her emotions for Charles. And, for years, Dominic had kept his mouth shut because his sister would not have been ready to hear what he had to say.

He had hoped Charles would win her heart, and knew, too, the man would cherish her and not treated as a prize for some title seeking, get rich schemer.

"Charles is a grown man, Rose. I'm sure he knows what he's doing." God, I hope so, Dominic thought. He wasn't sure Charles realized the implications of being seen with another woman in front of her. Then again, this move might turn out to be the smartest thing Charles has ever done in trying to finally capture his sister's attention.

"Come along, Rose," he told her, standing up and reaching out a hand to assist her. "If monsieur Forshaw is coherent, I am sure he will want to apologize for causing your distress."

The confusion clear on her face, she asked, "What happened to him? He looked perfectly fine, moments ago."

Dominic's lip quirked upward into a half-smile. "He upset you, and you left him alone with our father and your protective brothers."

Her eyes bulged. They wouldn't.… "Oh, mon Dieu!" she cried, leaping to her feet. She ran back to her study, afraid of what she would discover there.

She found her family reclining in chairs, speaking with each other. But Rudolph Forshaw was nowhere in sight.

"Where is he?" she asked, looking frantically from one brother to the next.

"Who?" her father asked.

"Randolph!" she exclaimed.

"Rudolph," Dominic gently corrected.

Theodore waved a hand in the air as though he deemed the question unimportant. "We killed him and buried the body behind the guest house," he answered nonchalantly.

Rosalinda's eyes bulged. "You did what?!"

Her father got to his feet and stared at her. "I find it troubling you would believe we could do such a thing," he told her.

Grimacing, she looked away. Their father had always reprimanded with facial expressions rather than physical actions. As a child, whenever that look crossed his face, she had felt his disappointment to her very core, and now was no exception. Her siblings were not murderers. They might beat someone within an inch of their lives if they felt the situation warranted it, but they would not kill them. "I apologize," she murmured.

Theodore stood and walked toward her. "The man is on his way to collect some of his belongings," he explained. "He will be back this afternoon." Reaching up, he gently tucked a stray lock of hair behind her ear. "Are you all right, Rose?"

Throat tight with emotion, knowing they loved her unconditionally, she nodded.

"Rose," Theodore's voice broke through to her inner thoughts.

She focused on him; smiled. "I am sorry. What were you saying?"

"We are all hungry and thought you would like to join us somewhere for lunch. Do you have any preferences where we should dine?"

The name of a restaurant slipped through her lips as though they had a life of their own. She did not dwell on why it was essential to visit

Paris's oldest dining room. But it seemed almost as critical as taking her next breath that she did.

Without giving thought to it, she rushed up the stairs to dress for the outing.

Chapter Seven

One did not walk into La Tour d'Argent and expect to obtain a seat at a table without having a reservation.

Located on the banks of the River Seine, between Notre Dame Cathedral and the Jardin des Plantes, La Tour d'Argent famously claims its establishment dates back to 1582. They even boast that King Henri IV was a regular patron—some say he even learned to use a fork there. However, this claim is problematic: the Quai de Tournelle, where the restaurant sits, was not paved until 1650. Therefore, whether Henri IV was actually a customer remains very much in question.

Having begun as a cheap boarding house with a restaurant serving staples of steak and house red wines, it became, over the years, the go-to place for the rich and famous. Regular patrons had included Marilyn Monroe, John Wayne, and Queen Elizabeth II of England, and famous writers, like San and Balzac.

A dinner, honoring Orville and Wilbur Wright, took place there in 1906.

It closed during the French Revolution in 1789. A decade later Napoleon Bonaparte's private chef, Monsieur Lecoq, brought back to life.

To get a table on the same day without a booking was not impossible. But your bank account would suffer for it.

Rosalinda beamed a radiant smile at her father as the Maitre d' escorted the group of six toward the restaurant's enormous wrap-around bay windows, where the picture-perfect view Of Notre Dame and the Seine took one's breath away. "Thank you, Papa." She said.

Albert Vallombrosa took his daughter's hand and tucked it into the crook of his arm. His look was full of affection, as he said, "I should make you pay the price they charged me for this table."

She smiled at him and knew he wasn't serious about taking her funds.

They had not had reservations.

Her eyes roamed the room. But she was not taking in the spectacular view of Paris that the wrap-around windows revealed. Nor was she looking at the elegant grand salon with the sea of servers hustling about. She was not sure why she hoped to see Charles there, but something was nudging her to look for him.

"Rosalinda! Rosalinda! Over here! Look, Charles! Can you believe Rosalinda Vallombrosa is here at La Tour d'Argent?"

All conversation halted in the restaurant. Many eyes turned to see if they could find the person who was making a spectacle of themselves. And, perhaps, to see if the famous starlet was among them. Although, if she were, they would not intrude. The French would not behave so foolishly in public as the woman in the white pillbox hat, which was no longer in fashion. She was standing up from her table and waving across the room.

The Vallombrosa hoard stopped their forward motion. They drew their attention to the table where Charles Lafayette was looking a little uncomfortable. But he plastered a smile on his face as he pushed away from the table and greeted the group. He shook hands with each Vallombrosa, then gave a slight bow to Rosalinda. "It is good to see you," he told them as a group, eyes lingering on Rosalinda for only a beat before he motioned toward the two women at the table with him.

Fortunately, conversation in the room started back up, as one by one, people dismissed the incident.

For the benefit of Albert, Theodore, Leopold, and Frederic, Charles said, "Please, allow me to introduce you to my special guests, Aimée-Louise Fontaine, and her mother, Lilith Fontaine. They are from the United States, visiting our country."

Rosalinda glanced at the older woman. The mother reminded her of a shriveled-up raisin. If the woman had been attractive in her youth, she had lost the glamour a long time ago. It was an uncharitable thought, but for the life of her, Rosalinda could not find it within herself to be sorry for it. Something about the mother did not bode well with her. At the moment, the woman was not looking all too happy to have suddenly had this interruption.

Aimée-Louise beamed. "It is so nice to meet all of you!" She butchered the French language enough to cause the Vallombrosa brood to switch to English for her benefit. And, to save the patrons within earshot, from hearing her horrible accent.

Albert gave a slight nod. "Oui. It is good to make your acquaintance." He looked at his children and said, "I believe our table is waiting."

Rosalinda gave Aimée-Louise a radiant smile. Regardless of the fact, she was grinding her teeth at the doe-eyed look she witnessed the woman make at Charles. "It is a pity we could not join you," Rosalinda said.

It was a suggestive tone, and she hoped the woman would take the bait. Rosalinda refused to sit by while this woman and her scarecrow of a mother did whatever it was they were doing. Something did not seem right about the pair. And the starlet's protectiveness toward Charles was kicking into overdrive.

For the briefest of moments, Aimée-Louise looked relieved. But the expression vanished as quickly as it had come, and she looked at her mother, and told the woman, "I think that would be a lovely idea! Perhaps this establishment would allow us to move tables together? I would love to have lunch with Rosalinda!"

Lilith looked as though she would choke. She sputtered, "I am sure Miss Vallombrosa would much rather spend time with her family, rather than with us, dear. She does not know us…"

Rosalinda waved her hand, "Nonsense! What better way to become acquainted than over lunch?"

Dominic leaned toward his sister, whispered in her ear. "You understand this game, whatever it is, will be very, very expensive." If the restaurant accommodated them, this already pricey affair would cost a small fortune.

Rosalinda gave him such an innocent look, he could have almost believed she was guiltless, had he not known her so well.

The Maitre d' glanced around the room, speculating the financial gain. Besides, nothing was impossible if one had enough funds to cover the price.

"Rosalinda," her father warned, as he calculated the sum of indulging his youngest child. He never minded spending his funds for his children's birthday celebrations, nor showering them with gifts at Christmas. He had enough funds to do whatever he wished. But, other than their birthdays and Christmas, he preferred spending his funds wisely. And this was not a wise investment, as far as he was concerned.

"Oh, but papa!" she cried, eyes wide and pleading, "She is visiting from America! It would be grand to know her better!"

"Invite her to your house for coffee if you wish to socialize with her," Theodore grumbled.

Charles looked at the Maitre d'. "I will cover the cost if you can make the arrangements," he promised. "And we shall have the 3-course Prix fixe lunch."

Beaming with the knowledge the meal alone would total well above five hundred dollars, the Maitre d' began clapping his hands together and barking out orders to the waiters, as he instructed tables to be reset. La Tour d'Argent was most definitely going to be profitable on this day.

Aimée-Louise squealed with her delight. Her mother, though, looked as though she was ready to spit.

That alone gave Rosalinda great gratification.

Everyone except for Lilith moved out of the way. The old hag sat in her chair, forcing the staff to work around her as they reset the arrangement.

Aimée-Louise leaned into Charles, wrapped her arms around him, and kissed him on the cheek. "Oh, thank you, darling!" she exclaimed, beaming at him.

The show of affection made Rosalinda's heart clench. What could Charles possibly see in that tart? Her irritation instantly escalated to anger when she saw the look of satisfaction flash across Lilith's face as the mother watched the embrace.

Once the staff finished setting the table and everyone began taking a seat, Rosalinda quickly wedged herself between Aimée-Louise and

Charles. She cast her own small smile of vindication toward the old hag, who looked away with a sniff.

Ignoring the mother, Rosalinda turned her attention to Aimée-Louise. However, she was very much aware of Charles sitting on her right. It had been hard not to stare at him. He seemed more handsome, in the light of day, than he had last night. How was that possible?

"So, tell me, Aimée-Louise," Rosalinda said, focusing in on the blond bimbo, "What brings you to Paris?"

Aimée-Louise picked up her napkin, set it in her lap. "Oh! It was mother's idea!" she gushed, "She thought it would be grand to tour this marvelous city, and I believe she is right. I am having a wonderful time! I was fortunate to have bumped into Charles not long after we arrived in the city. My mother is a fan of his movies and had hoped to meet him before we left Paris."

Rosalinda leaned forward and glanced directly at the old woman. "Wasn't that fortunate of you?" she asked coolly, immediately wondering what the woman's scheme was. If it had anything to do with Charles's fame and fortune, Rosalinda would scratch their eyes out.

Rosalinda determined she would force these two out of Charles's life. Besides, having dated no one before, it was obvious the man did not know how to choose the right woman. Rosalinda knew exactly who the right woman was for him: she was sitting right here beside him. Although she hadn't figured out how to tell the man she had rejected year after year that she loved him, she knew she would not sit by and watch him make a fool of himself.

While Aimée-Louise conversed with Rosalinda, Charles glanced across the table to Dominic and grinned.

Dominic could only shake his head. It was apparent Charles was playing a game. If Dominic were a betting man, he would bet his friend was directing a live play, with no one being the wiser to the story he was weaving.

Secretly, Dominic was cheering the man on. His sister could be incredibly happy with the movie producer, and he would cherish her more than riches.

As the meal progressed, the conversation turned to the inauguration of the Mont Blanc Tunnel, a highway tunnel under the Mont Blanc mountain in the Alps. The tunnel would aid in transporting freight be-tween counties, as it reduced the route from France to Turin, Italy, by 30 miles. Everyone at the table was in favor of the tunnel.

Charles turned to Rosalinda and inquired, "Are you enjoying your day with your family?"

His rich, copper-colored eyes held her captive. She no longer questioned her attraction; she knew it was his kind nature and giving heart. He possessed a gentleness she had never known in a man outside of her own family. Charles was firm but utterly fair. On his film sets over the years, she had watched him warmly greet everyone he passed—from the garbage collector to the star of the show. He labeled no one above anyone else. That said, he was no pushover. He had an aura of command, demanded perfection, and would quickly set a person straight— or fire them—if they messed up too often. Those fortunate enough to work for him always gave their absolute best.

She blinked, instantly breaking whatever spell he had woven over her. "Mostly, oui," she replied. "They upset me this morning, hiring a body-guard without my permission. But I have forgiven them." An intense desire gripped her: she wanted to lean in, feel his strength, and breathe in the cologne that reminded her of a spring morning and daffodils after the rain. But she dared not—not yet. She needed to be alone with him before she confessed what a fool she had been.

His smile was warm and gentle. "You are loved very much."

Rosalinda almost leaned in and pressed her lips to his.

"Rosalinda? Are you listening to me?"

Rosalinda blinked, finally focusing on Aimée-Louise, who was waving a hand practically in her face. "I told you I was looking forward to seeing you at the party Charles and I are hosting tomorrow night. Our party will be grand, just grand." Aimée-Louise's smile was radiant.

Staring, Rosalinda repeated, "Your party?" Her mind seemed to stutter on the word our. Had Charles become so involved with this woman al-ready that they considered themselves a couple? Had she already lost

him? Had she acknowledged to herself that he was her very air, too late? It felt as though her heart would break. She had been a fool. A complete fool, to have denied him her love when he deserved so much more from her.

Beaming, Aimée-Louise nodded. "Yes. It will be fabulous! I believe Charles mentioned it last night when we visited you in your dressing room after the play."

Feeling her throat tighten, Rosalinda murmured, "I look forward to it." But she felt tears burning behind her eyes.

"Wonderful! Of course, you are welcome to bring a date. We are also expecting Brigitte Bardot, Jean Seberg, Michel Serrault, and even Fernandel!" She continued listing names she believed would attend, but Rosalinda heard none of them.

Our party. Theirs.

The room felt too hot and stuffy, despite it being a perfect temperature.

Looking up, Rosalinda saw Rudolph Forshaw near the front of the room, lingering with his hands in his pockets, trying to look as though he belonged there. Apparently, her family had contacted him before they left her home and let him know where they would be.

Pushing away from the table, Rosalinda stood up and glanced at her brothers. Concern for her was clear on their faces when they noticed she looked a little pale. Hastily she said, "Forgive me. I have an appointment." Her eyes met with Charles' and lingered.

Before she gave in to the tears threatening to appear, she rushed from the room, with Rudolph Forshaw trailing behind her.

Rendered speechless, the Vallombrosa clan stared after her, confusion clear on their faces.

Aimée-Louise's eyes were wide. "Well!" She exclaimed. "That was very rude of her."

Lilith sat back in her chair, contemplating, knowing this might benefit her, or ruin everything she had been working towards. It was just her luck to have a simpleton for a daughter.

As Charles watched Rosalinda rush from the room, he almost went after her but forced himself to sit there. He could not believe how well this whole thing was going, and he needed to see it through.

He caught Aimée-Louise's eye when no one was looking, and a slight smile crossed his lips.

Outside La Tour d'Argent, Rosalinda walked aimlessly, seeing nothing of her surroundings. She simply lacked the emotional strength to stop and acknowledge the people who recognized her and called out her name. She did not notice Rudolph keeping a short distance behind her, warding off anyone from approaching her. Head down, her mind flashed painful images of Charles. Was it too late to tell him what she felt? Would he accept her declaration of love after years of rejection? She had refused him because she didn't want to settle down—and now, here she was, ready to give him everything.

Now that she knew he was her very breath; she might lose him. And she had no one to blame but herself.

Stopping along the walkway, she stared out at the River Seine, brushing frantically at the tears she could no longer hold back. She was twenty-seven years old, and she couldn't fight the emotions she had harbored for Charles all these years. Why had she been so foolish? Everything she had ever longed for in a man had been right there, in front of her, the entire time.

With her mind instantly made up, she spun around quickly and slammed right into Rudolph, who had been standing just behind her, anticipating her next move. She would have lost her balance and landed on her backside if he hadn't swiftly caught her by the shoulders.

"Forgive me, Randolph," she apologized, almost embarrassed by the mishap.

Rudolph debated for two seconds whether he should correct her regarding his name, before deeming it a lost cause. For whatever reason, the starlet seemed not to care if she said his name correctly or not. It did not matter. Not really. With the hefty salary her family was paying him to keep her safe, she could call him anything she liked.

"No harm done," he said, removing his hands from her shoulders and putting them to his sides. "I was standing too closely; now tell me, where would you like to go, and I shall escort you there."

She looked down the street toward La Tour d'Argent in time to see Charles' limousine pulled to the curb, and he and the two women climb inside.

Rosalinda squared her shoulders. She would not give up Charles without a fight. But she needed time to plan and think.

"Home," she told the bodyguard, "You may take me home."

Tomorrow she would go to Charles; once she had a firm grasp on what she would say to the man. Tonight, however, she had another performance at the playhouse and needed to prepare herself to fall into character.

Chapter Eight

That evening, as Rosalinda performed the last act of the play, she was glad she knew the part as though it were second nature.

She hadn't been able to take her focus off Charles. Throughout the day, she tried and almost debated having her under-study take over for her tonight, so she could take care of this matter of her heart. But if nothing else, Rosalinda was a professional. She had never been one to pass her duty onto someone else unless she was too sick to perform. And being sick at heart was not a worthy cause to excuse herself from the play.

Now on stage, about to deliver the dramatic line that would cause the audience to hold their breath in anticipation, she paused. It was at this point in the play when Rosalinda was to pick up a prop gun and aim it at her leading man Andy, as she confronted her on stage lover for having had an affair.

Rosalinda had almost reached the table holding the prop gun when she glanced into the audience. She didn't understand why she did it—this was not how she had ever delivered this part of the script before. But something had caught her eye, pulling her focus for a critical moment. Distractions never happened to her, yet it was happening now.

Maybe, she reasoned, she had been hoping to see Charles sitting in the front row again tonight. Or, perhaps, she wanted the thrill of looking upon the sea of people watching the drama about to unfold. Knowing they would hold their breath in anticipation because they knew she was about to shoot her lover.

People had a morbid obsession with death.

The quick view of the spectators warmed her heart. But, as she looked away, her eyes chanced upon a man sitting in the front row, nearest the aisle. She stumbled, catching herself by reaching out and holding onto the small table on the stage. Heart drumming in her ears, she focused on the man sitting there staring back at her with malice on his face and she

became frozen in place. Her mind could not accept what her eyes were seeing.

Murmuring amongst the audience began, as their favorite actress stayed rooted in place. They could not understand why she was looking their way and not continuing with the production.

Something wasn't right.

The man who held Rosalinda's focus slowly stood up. The smile he gave her wasn't friendly. It only promised pain. Then he saluted her, stepped into the aisle and quickly made his way up the walkway, exiting the arena before she could cry out.

As though in a dream, she felt her body slowly slide to the floor as pandemonium broke out around her. Andy rushed forward, trying to catch her before she hit the ground. The audience moved restlessly. Some of them remained in their seats, while others stood up to get a better view of what was transpiring on stage.

Walter ran onto the stage, demanding the curtains be lowered.

Rudolph, who also had been standing off stage, moved with lightning speed past Walter. He reached Rosalinda, knelt by her side as he began examining her. "What is it?" he asked frantically. "Have you been in- jured?" He wondered what could explain her collapsing on stage. Had something physical caused her to do so?

Rosalinda looked at him, terror in her eyes. "Pierre," she managed in a whisper, "Pierre Bellefeuille is here!"

Kneeling, Walter said, "Rosalinda, what are you talking about? The man is in prison."

She shook her head, stared past the lowering curtains. "No! I saw him! He was sitting in the audience."

Walter shook his head. "Perhaps it was only a man who resembles him."

Rosalinda trembled. "No! It was Pierre!"

"How can that be?" Walter asked and repeated, "The man is in prison."

She grabbed his hand. "And I am telling you; he is not!"

For only a moment, Walter hesitated. Unsure what to do. It was obvious something had deeply troubled Rosalinda. She was not a woman to make up something as horrific as this.

"Drop the curtain!" Walter snapped out when he noticed part of the curtain remained open. Then he yelled to no one in particular, "Call the police!"

Rudolph helped the shaken actress to her feet.

"Come," Rudolph told her, placing a hand in the small of her back, "We shall go to your dressing room and wait for the authorities to arrive."

Rosalinda's body vibrated with fear. The dread was tangible. She followed Rudolph as though in a dream. If it wasn't for him holding her hand, as he made way for her to reach her dressing room, she would not have known the correct path to take.

How could it be true? How could Pierre possibly be free?

Oh God, her heart squeezed in fear. It was apparent why he had allowed her to see him. He wanted her to know he would come for her. Of that, she was certain. He was not a man who forgave someone he believed had worked against him. Even though she had only a small part in hiding Jacqueline from him, he wanted his form of justice.

* * *

While Rosalinda performing on stage, Inspector Thomas Levegue stood near the bank of Paris's oldest bridge, examining the gruesome scene his chief had unfortunately assigned to him. The sick green colored water flowing under Pont Neuf bridge caused him a slight grimace.

The fact of the Seine River being the primary water source for Paris had not escaped him. It did not matter if the water went through filtration and cleansing before being deemed safe to consume. Looking at it in its original state, with the decomposing body his men were pulling from it, turned his stomach. Knowing where the water came from used to make the coffee, he was sipping was enough to have him tossing the remaining brew into a nearby bush.

He wondered how long it would be before he would want a drink of water again.

"Sir, I have the man who found the body. He is in my car. Did you want to question him now?"

Levegue sighed. Did he want to? No. Absolutely not, but it was all part of the job. "Do something with this," he said, pushing the empty cup into the officer's hand before walking in the direction where the poor guy waited in the patrol car. The man had been walking his dog; never dreaming he would find a dead person floating face up.

Seeing a crowd gathering, trying to push forward to view the victim, had Levegue snarling. He roared at one of the low-ranking officers to move the people back or face a firing squad.

Vultures, that's all they were. The bystanders, lurking around for information they could use later to gossip with friends when the news regarding the poor woman became public knowledge.

She had been murdered and dumped in the Seine. This was not a suicide. He had seen the body. Someone had tortured her. That person had sliced her up as though she had been a Thanksgiving turkey. Her face…

He shuddered and knew he would have nightmares in the days to come. Not only had the fish fed off her flesh, but someone had had great fun cutting her eyes out.

Already, in his mind was the fact Pierre Bellefeuille had escaped from maximum security the previous night. He could not help but wonder if this victim had unfortunately met the man.

The night had turned into a major pain in his ass.

With a sigh, Levegue walked past the now dispersing crowd, ascended the walkway leading to the upper street, and made his way to the police car.

The man, who had been luckless enough to discover the horrendous scene, was sitting in the back of the patrol car, the man's mutt next to him. Levegue doubted he would learn anything from the blubbering guy or his drooling dog, but he had procedure to follow. Levegue had not spent fifteen years with the police department by sidestepping duty.

Red-rimmed eyes, caused by the man's distress at having found a dead body, looked up when the shadow of Levegue fell on him. "It is horrible!" the man sobbed on a hiccup.

Levegue nodded. "Yes, it is. Unfortunately, murder normally is dreadful. Could you tell me how you found the victim?"

"Daisy….., she found the" the man trembled, "She is the one who found the woman." At the memory, the man began blubbering all over again.

Levegue sighed and felt a headache coming on. He hated this part of questioning witnesses. If they would tell you straight out what happened, instead of allowing emotions to rule, he could move on to another part of the investigation. But it never worked out that way. So, he had to prod the man by asking, "And Daisy would be….?"

The man threw his arms around the long-haired breed of questionable origins setting next to him.

Exhaling a breath, Levegue figured he knew who Daisy was; his eyes roamed over the golden-brown fur of the beast he suspected owned the name.

With the patience of a saint, Levegue questioned the sobbing idiot. Every answer came out on a sob. No, he did not know the woman. Yes, he and Daisy walked this way every evening. No, he had seen no one around when Daisy began barking at something in the water.

Inspector Levegue covered every question he could think of, knowing this man, and his flowery dog did not have the answers he was looking for. When he was through with the interview, he motioned to another officer standing close by. "You can take him home. I'm done here."

Levegue watched the man and his pet disappear in the patrol car.

As the vehicle rolled forward, Levegue felt someone come up behind him. He turned and faced the person standing there. "Hell of a night," he commented to the man, then began walking back to where the ambulance personnel were wrapping the woman's body for its trip to the morgue. He hoped the coroner could identify the victim quickly. Although, from what he had seen of her, there had been little of her face left to help the process along.

He felt a shudder run through him. Wondering again, if it was pure coincidence that Pierre Bellefeuille was on the loose and that a woman's body had been found this evening.

Inspector General Arthur Banvard fell into step with Levegue.

"Have you got any leads?" the inspector asked.

Levegue stopped, turned, and met his boss's eyes. "Someone killed her," he said dryly. Good God! He had only been on the job thirty minutes, and already the Inspector General thought he should have answers.

The glare Banvard shot his way had not been unexpected but damn it; investigations into murder took time.

"All right Art," Levegue said, using his superior's first name, angrily throwing his arms out to his sides in frustration, "you want to know what I think? This has the smell of Bellefeuille all over it. What I cannot grasp is why he would break out of prison and come to Paris? I would think he would leave the country as soon as possible, not risk coming here of all places. He knows we would look for him under every rock."

"No one has ever understood Bellefeuille." Banvard shrugged as he followed in step with Levegue as he began walking again. "I have to tell you; my office receive communication from an American agency. The man heading up the organization is the agent who helped transport Bellefeuille here from the United States a few years ago. During that time, we agreed to keep him informed of anything pertaining to Pierre."

Thomas Levegue spit in the grass. He was not a fan of anyone who wasn't French.

Banvard shook his head, knowing this man would not like what he had to say next. "Because of our agreement, we contacted his office immediately upon discovering Pierre had escaped prison."

Levegue cycled his finger in the air. "Everyone must be happy now that your people contacted their people. It has nothing to do with my investigation."

"I am letting you know; you might have to team up with the man when he arrives."

Levegue stopped, sneered. "I know how to do my job. I do not need some damn American sticking his nose in my business."

Banvard chuckled. Thomas Levegue had never liked Americans. "The two of you will cooperate." He was not giving assurance; it was an order, and Levegue knew it.

"Bah," Thomas said, and began walking away. When the American arrived, the man had better stay out of his way.

Banvard laughed. "In the meantime, his office called to inform us we are to send officers to guard Rosalinda Vallombrosa immediately."

That caused Levegue to stop short. Turning, he clarified in a sneer, "The actress?"

Banvard put his hand on his heart, as though smitten. "My dear friend, there can only be one Rosalinda Vallombrosa."

"You are old enough to be her grandfather."

"I may be old, but that does not mean I cannot appreciate a beautiful woman."

Shaking his head, Levegue would not comment. He asked instead, "What is Vallombrosa to Pierre?"

"Her best friend was his stepsister."

"Was?"

"Bellefeuille had her murdered." That was what he had been told. Only a hand full of people knew the truth that Jacqueline was alive and well and living in the United States.

With a sigh, Levegue began walking again. Resources were thin already. Now, they expected him to dispatch men to guard an actress just because she was unfortunate enough to have chosen the wrong friend. Ridiculous.

"Rosalinda helped his stepsister elude him for a time. The American agent believes Pierre will want revenge because of it."

Levegue shuddered; he did not want to think what could happen to the actress if Bellefeuille had her in his twisted sights.

"I will send someone as soon as I can," Levegue told him.

"I have already done so," Banvard informed him. He hoped they would not need the men, and Bellefeuille had long since left the country.

Chapter Nine

Rosalinda's dressing room had never felt smaller than it did while she waited for the authorities to arrive. Rudolph stood by the door, keeping everyone out, while Walter fussed over her as though she were a delicate flower. Yes, she had collapsed earlier on stage, because of the unexpected sight of Pierre sitting with the audience. But that was then, and this was now and, "Walter, please give me some air to breathe!" she exclaimed, rubbing at her temples.

Feeling rejected, Walter sat down on the only other chair in the room, an uncomfortable swivel chair, which had no support for his back. "I was only trying to help," he grumbled, looking away from her.

"I appreciate it," she now was the one to soothe. And she would have laughed at Walter's childish dejected expression, if she weren't so terrified. "I need you here... I just cannot have you hovering over me."

Sniffling, he looked away from her.

With a sigh, Rosalinda looked to Rudolph for help. The bodyguard shrugged, and she knew no help would come from that direction. She decided her best course of action was to close the door on the subject. Walter wanted to sulk, so she would let him. She had deadly matters to occupy herself with.

How was it possible that Pierre was out of prison? She was petrified and did not know where to turn.

She would not call Jacqueline and Colten. She would not contact them. Knowing if she did, Pierre would somehow discover the truth and go after them. No, she would cause nothing to happen to the Fisher family if it were within her power.

What was taking the police so long to get here? Did they not understand what sort of man Pierre was?

The knowledge that he could be, at this moment, hiding outside, waiting for her to leave the building, frightened her. If the police would but

hurry, then perhaps they could find him quickly and put him back behind bars.

It took the police almost forty-five minutes before they arrived at the playhouse; two officers, along with a man in a black trenchcoat, who introduced himself as Inspector Levegue.

"My apologies, Mademoiselle," Levegue told her. "We sent men to your home as soon as we were told to do so." He shrugged, at a loss. They should have thought of sending men to both her home and here. But he'd had other things on his mind. And no one expected Bellefeuille to be bold enough to reveal himself so publicly. Which was a foolish assumption. Bellefeuille was never predictable.

"There has been no announcement anywhere!" Walter exclaimed. "There has been nothing about his escape on the news, radio, or newspaper. The public has the right to know when a dangerous criminal is at large! At least Rosalinda would have been prepared!"

"We had no reason to believe Mademoiselle Vallombrosa was in danger, and we kept his escape quite for our own reasons."

"It is no excuse!" Walter shouted.

Rosalinda raised her hand to stop the building argument. "Inspector Levegue, perhaps you could contact someone for me. He is an American agent who is very aware of the danger I could be in, and he is more than familiar with Pierre."

"I already have one American agent on his way from the United States; I do not need another one to interfere with my investigation."

Rosalinda stood. "Who? Who is coming? What is their name?" And although Colten Fisher had retired from Cadman's agency, she hoped he would not be foolish enough to put himself in danger. He had a family now, and they needed him.

"Cadman Benson," Levegue answered.

Closing her eyes, almost swooning with relief, Rosalinda wrapped her arms around herself, feeling a small sense of safety knowing Cadman was on his way to Paris. "Thank you," she told Levegue.

Cocking an eye, Levegue asked, "Why are you thanking me?"

"Cadman Benson is the man I wanted you to contact. He will know what to do." She trusted Cadman with her life.

Grinding his teeth at what he considered an insult, Levegue snapped out orders to the two officers with him, telling one of them to take the starlet home and stand guard.

As Rudolph, and one officer, escorted Rosalinda to the waiting patrol car, Rudolph asked her, "This Cadman Benson you mentioned. You trust him?"

Sliding into the backseat of the vehicle, Rudolph entering after her, she said, "Absolutely." She would always trust Cadman to know what to do.

But, as the patrol car pulled away from the curb, it was not Cadman Benson who occupied Rosalinda's thoughts. Staring at the back of the young officer's head, she contemplated. She would rather not go home. That would be a natural place for Pierre to find her, if he was seeking her out to cause her harm. She thought about going to her parents' home, or to the home of one of her siblings, but dismissed those ideas. Rosalinda would feel suffocated. No, she longed for the comfort of someone else and told the officer, "Turn around. I want you to drive me to the Lafayette mansion."

The officer glanced at her in the rear-view mirror. "I have orders to take you home."

"Damn your orders!" she snapped. "You can tell your inspector where I am, but I refuse to go home."

The man looked torn between following a direct order from his superior or accommodating his passenger. But, after a minute, he made a U-turn, pointing the cruiser in the direction of the movie producer's home.

Upon arrival, they saw lights on in the mansion and knew that someone was up at this hour of eleven pm. The officer stopped the car and opened the door for Rosalinda. Rudolph exited from the opposite side.

Rosalinda rang the bell, and they waited. It wasn't long before Charles's butler opened the door.

Rosalinda inquired, "Is Charles in residence?"

Heath, a man who had been employed by Charles for the past ten years, smiled. He had always had a secret crush on the woman who was twenty years his junior "Mademoiselle Vallombrosa, as always, it is a pleasure to see you." He did not question her standing at the door at this late hour, too accustomed to his employer having late at night meetings. Often those meetings were regarding the backlot his studio had purchased or the demolition of the abandoned neighborhood that would begin as soon as Sunday morning. "Monsieur Lafayette is in the living room with guests. Please wait here, and I will let him know you are here."

It wasn't long before Charles entered the foyer to greet them. When he saw Rosalinda's pale face, he became concerned. She appeared frightened, which was unusual. Rosalinda had always been a woman who knew what she wanted and went after her dreams; damning the consequences. There had only been one time he had ever seen her shaken, and with that memory, apprehension began. "Rosalinda, what is it?" He glanced from the officer to Rudolph, then back to her. "What is wrong?"

Hovering behind him, she saw Lilith and Aimée-Louise. Knowing Pierre was free, and no doubt after her, Rosalinda's resentment rose.

Lilith did not look pleased. Rosalinda hoped she had ruined the night for the two women. God knew hers had been devastated. Seeing Aimée-Louise here, at this hour, only caused her heart to squeeze tight.

Rosalinda felt as though her world was quickly falling apart.

"May we speak in private?" Rosalinda asked Charles, moving her attention away from the two women before she did something drastic, which would cause both woman physical pain.

With a nod, Charles ushered her toward his study; a room filled with rich leather and wood furniture. A decorative ceiling drew the eye, while the red Venetian plaster walls added more texture to the room. Soft lighting gave the room a feeling of calm. There were floor-to-ceiling drapes and an area rug that tied all the colors of the room together. One wall was lined with a massive bookcase. She decided this room could be her favorite place to relax. Which was precisely what she needed at this grim time.

He closed the door, then turned and waited for Rosalinda to speak. It was difficult to remain still—to not step forward, embrace her, and offer comfort when she was clearly in distress. He resisted but ached desperately to hold her.

The desire to do so almost overwhelmed him.

She walked around the room, hand trailing over the leather of one chair, then slowly, she faced him.

"Why is Aimée-Louise here?" She had not meant to ask the question, but she had and was not sorry for it.

He shook his head, moving to a nearby chair and sat on the arm. "You surprise me, Rosalinda. Although I do not owe you an explanation, I will give you one." He stood back up and moved to his desk, playing with a pen that lay on top of it. His heart pulsated. Could she possibly be jealous? After all these years, had he unlocked the key that would draw her to him?

Dare he hope?

Calmly he told her, "We dined together and completed plans for tomorrow's party."

Her heart twisted. The thought of having lost him to another woman, had her saying bluntly, "You do realize she, or at the very least, her mother, is probably after your money and fame."

He did not know why he was suddenly so angry, but he was. He threw the pen onto the desk and stocked toward her. It was so unlike him to show anger, Rosalinda found herself retreating backward until her back encountered a wall, and she could not move any farther.

"Rosalinda, I have loved you for years! Years!" he shouted, instantly regretting yelling when he desperately wanted to hold her. "You probably know that; it's not as though I've made it a secret. Because of that love, I never commented on your loose ways, but it wasn't my place to! We had no personal relationship. You are clearly not interested in what I offer, whether you find me inadequate or simply aren't attracted to me. But by God, don't you dare stand there and judge someone I choose to spend time with!" He stepped forward until his shoes touched hers. "I

recently decided I needed to move on. I gave up hope that you would ever see me as a man."

She stared into his eyes, so full of emotion. She wanted to weep, for all the pain she had caused him, and for the foolish notion of not to settling for one man.

He was the only man in the world for her.

A tear trickled down her cheek as she whispered. "Do not," she choked out, "Do not give up on me!"

Heart pounding, Charles stared. "What are you saying?" His voice was an emotional whisper. Desperately, he wanted her to say the words he had always longed to hear.

Words failed her; they simply would not pass her lips. Instead, she raised her hands, threaded them around Charles's neck, and pulled his face down to hers. Their lips met, entwining in a deep, enticing kiss. This was what she had always longed for—the truth that had been right in front of her all these years. The feel of his mouth on hers instantly fed a hunger that had remained unsatisfied until this moment.

Someone moaned; neither of them cared who made the sound. They were too caught up in the electric current created by their body contact to care.

Rosalinda's hands roamed freely down his shirt, finding the tiny buttons. Without breaking contact from his mouth, she undid enough buttons to allow her hand to slip in and run her fingertips over the soft hair of his chest. She marveled at how broad and exquisitely sculpted it felt, making her wonder what he looked like under that gray suit he wore.

Her breathing grew heavy as their tongues tasted desire, and hands explored each other.

"My God," Charles gasped. His hand slipped into the top of her dress, tracing the curve of her breast, and then gently squeezed her aroused nipple. "My God," he repeated in a ragged whisper, taking her mouth in a consuming kiss. Actually holding her was better than any dream he'd spent years wishing for. Now that she was here, he didn't want this to end.

It took a noticeable moment for the entwined couple to hear the sound of someone knocking at the door.

Startled by the knocking, they pulled away from each other. His copper-colored eyes collided with her unique green ones. They looked guilty, as though someone had caught them in a trespass.

"Rosalinda!" It was Rudolph calling her name.

She looked at the door. "One moment!" she called back, hastily righting her clothing, as Charles made quick work of buttoning his shirt. He looked at her and could not be sorry for their encounter. But he regretted the interruption with a glaring passion.

It did, however, prompt him to remember that she had arrived at his door with her bodyguard and an officer of the law. "What has happened?"

The question was like a splash of icy water to her body. It quickly sobered her fevered sexual state. "Bellefeuille has escaped," she told him. "I need your help."

Chapter Ten

He would do anything to keep her safe.

It felt as though he had been abruptly transported into a nightmare. Moments earlier, Rosalinda was in his arms—a fantasy finally come true. His mind was still reeling with the knowledge of her love and desire. But now, a threat to her life could snatch away their happily ever after, and he flatly refused to let it happen. Pierre Bellefeuille was not a man who allowed loose ends to slip through his fingers. Because Pierre let Rosalinda see him, Charles was now certain, as sure as he needed air to breathe, that the man would come after her.

Raising his hand, Charles stroked her cheek. "Do you truly love me, Rosalinda?" He needed reassurance that she was not only there seeking shelter and a place to hide like before. Three years ago, when Bellefeuille was running free, she had stayed with him at his home in New York City, where he kept her hidden from the madman.

She could not fault him for questioning her motives. After all, she had waited until now to tell him her feelings. He had no idea she would have told him at his party tomorrow evening that she wanted to be with him.

Nodding, she whispered, "I think I fell in love with you on the day we first met. You will never know how sorry I am for suppressing that truth, even from myself. But, if you let me, I plan on spending the rest of my life showing you how much I cherish you."

If possible, his heart swelled even more. "And you will marry me?" He made it sound more like a decree and held his breath.

Rosalinda's smile lit up the room. "Oh yes, dear heart, I will marry you!" She could hardly believe she had not hesitated with her answer, but she meant what she said.

She would marry this man, the man who had always shown her patience and kindness, even when she had not deserved it. She would gladly be his wife.

The pounding on the door sounded a second time. "Rosalinda!" Rudolph called, "Is everything all right? Will you be staying? I need to plan with the authorities if you will reside here."

Charles glanced over his shoulder and called out, "She will indeed stay with me!" He was the happiest man in the world. Looking back at the love of his life, he asked, "Will you marry me tonight?" He was not about to let her slip through his fingers. Not now, not ever. She had to know he would accept nothing less than marriage.

God, he wished he wasn't so old-fashioned. He ached to have her in his bed. But morals, ingrained in the child he had been, were difficult to push aside. His stepfather had always taught him that true love should not be confused with sex.

He wanted to curse his stepfather for convincing him of that old-world view. Because, more than anything, Charles wanted to whisk this woman to his bed. But if she truly loved him, then she would marry him first.

On a laugh, she threw her arms around him. "Charles, if that is what you wish, I would marry you whenever you desire! My family will be distraught if they cannot hold a celebration, the likes Paris has never seen. But, if you can make the arrangements, it would honor me to become your wife this evening."

He crushed his mouth to hers and pulled her against him tight. "If you said that believing I could not make it happen, Rosalinda, you will be in for a surprise. I know people. Tonight is your wedding night! Your parents can plan the celebration of a lifetime later."

The door opened with a bang; Rudolph stepped in. He took one look at the tousled couple standing in the middle of the room and blushed. "Err... Forgive me..." He shoved his hands in his pockets. "I will let the police officer know all is well."

Charles laughed and looked at Rosalinda. "I need to let Aimée-Louise and her mother know the party is canceled and have my chauffeur take them to their hotel."

"You can still have your party." She told him, "But it is our party, and we will make it a small celebration, that is until my family can hold their

own extravaganza." She laughed, imagining the vast affair her parents would host. They had been waiting years for her to settle down and stop her careless ways.

"Do you think," Rosalinda asked, wrapping her arms around his waist, "Aimée-Louise will be disappointed that she will no longer be the hostess?"

"She never was the hostess," he grinned at his confession. "But, I did not mind letting you believe she was."

Rosalinda gasped. "You planned this?"

He shook his head. "I had hoped it would happen, but I did not know what the outcome would be."

"Charles Lafayette," Rosalinda chastised.

He grinned at her. "Now, darling. Let's not fight before the wedding."

He owed Aimée-Louise a great deal for having executed her part in the plan better than he could have hoped. Lilith, on the other hand, would not be pleased to discover her plans had been thwarted. He was grateful to Aimée-Louise for being an honest person, and nothing like her conniving mother. He would deal with Lilith another time. But for now, he had a wedding to put together quickly.

Together they walked back into the elegant foyer, with its beige walls, marble floors, curved staircase, and its double glass front door. Stopping in the entrance, Charles told Aimée-Louise and her mother, "Forgive me for keeping you waiting. I will have my chauffeur take you back to your hotel." He could not hold it in for another minute. "I am getting married tonight!" He wanted to shout it from the rooftops.

Aimée-Louise squealed with delight. She clapped her hands and exclaimed, "How wonderful!"

When Lilith wasn't looking, Charles silently mouthed, "Thank you," to Aimée-Louise. Upon seeing the gratitude in Charles' eye, she slightly tilted her head in acknowledgement.

A glance at Lilith gave Rosalinda so much pleasure, she almost stuck out her tongue at the old hag. The woman looked livid enough to kill. "We hope you will come to the party Charles and I are having tomorrow

night," Rosalinda said, in a voice laced with artificial sweetness. "We will announce our marriage to the guests." She gave Lilith an innocent look and hoped it grated the woman's nerves. Charles may believe Aimée-Louise was harmless, and perhaps she was, but her mother was another matter entirely. Rosalinda was not sure what it was about the woman that bothered her. But deep down, she sensed the old bat had been trying to play matchmaker between Charles and her daughter.

Whatever her intentions were, it was not because she cared about the movie producer. Rosalinda was convinced the two women were after Charles's fortune.

Lilith's smile was visibly forced. "Of course, we would be honored to attend," she managed. Turning to her daughter, she added, "We will have to shop tomorrow for a gift for the happy couple." The sarcasm in her tone was unmistakable.

Again Aimée-Louise clapped. "That is a wonderful idea, mother."

Lilith rolled her eyes.

Charles used the phone in the foyer to ring his chauffeur, then excused himself and Rosalinda. Taking her hand in his, he moved them back into the study.

Charles telephoned the people he knew, who could get the proper documents on such short notice and at this late hour. He had no qualms about getting the priest he knew out of bed. Although he was not a religious man, he made sizable donations to this church because of its work with the homeless. Father Delaveyne would be there within the hour to preside.

As he finished the last phone call, Charles stood, about to gather Rosalinda in his arms, still not believing she was about to be his bride, when a knock sounded at the door. Instead of reaching for his soon to be lover, he moved to open the door, finding his mother just on the other side, looking tired. Her bedroom was on the first floor. The sounds of the staff had awakened her as they were scurrying about, preparing for the impromptu wedding. She had retired early after the meal with Aimée-Louise, and Lilith had ended, not wishing to listen to the women's chatter. But now she stood there in the doorway, looking confused.

"Charles," she inquired, "What is going on? Why is the chef baking a small cake at this hour?" Her eyes traveled into the room and landed upon Rosalinda. His mother had not lived all these years without knowing what went on behind closed doors, between a man and woman, at this hour of the night. But since they did not look disheveled, she assumed her son had not been having sex. Thank God, she thought to herself, she would have been embarrassed beyond belief.

It wasn't that Charles had deliberately kept his plan to marry her tonight a secret; it had simply slipped his mind entirely to inform her.

Charles grinned. "Mother, I am glad you are awake. You will be able to witness the wedding."

Rosalinda walked toward the desk, picked up the phone. "I will call my family. I'm sure they can be here within the hour. I want them here, even if it is not the wedding they would have planned for me." She dialed the number to her parents' home on the outskirts of Paris as Charles explained everything to his mother.

"Married!" Patricia gasped, her eyes flying once more to Rosalinda, then back to her son. "Have you lost your mind?" She had nothing against Rosalinda. She liked the little gal but... "There are more proper ways to go about having a wedding!"

He patted her on the back. "We will have a larger celebration later. But tonight, we will wed. I will not allow Rosalinda to slip through my fingers, now that I know she loves me." His mind still reeled knowing that after all these years of waiting for the woman he loved, all it took was for him to be seen with another woman to bring Rosalinda around.

Patricia moved farther into the room, stopping before Rosalinda, who was calling her family members to join them for the happiest evening of her life. When the starlet hung up the phone, Patricia whispered in a hopeful tone, "Do you really love my son?" Patricia prayed it was true, all she had ever wanted was for her son to be happy. She could see by the way that he stood now, tall and proud, that he was feeling on top of the moon.

Rosalinda glanced at Patricia and then looked at Charles. "I love him with all my heart." It amazed her to realize how freeing it felt to

proclaim it. She meant what she said. She would devote her life to making him happy. He deserved nothing less.

It was half-past two in the morning, when those they had called arrived. The Vallombrosa's, Rosalinda's parents, brothers, and their wives were an impressive group as they appeared together; their children left at home with their nannies. No need to wake them up at such a late hour. Each of Rosalinda's brothers bombarded the couple with questions, asking if this was indeed what Rosalinda wanted. Congratulating Charles on winning her favor and assuring the couple they had their support. They all had known the pair would make a beautiful couple if Rosalinda would one day come to her senses.

Once the priest arrived, Dominic managed to pull Charles aside. "I never would have believed it possible," he told his old college friend, "but I'm genuinely pleased. You took a huge gamble with Rose's affections, and you won. You're a good man, Charles. There is absolutely no one else I'd rather see her married to."

Charles' throat tightened. "Thank you, Dominic. I will cherish her forever."

The priest inquired, "And where shall the vows be spoken?"

Charles was about to answer when his butler entered the room. With a slight bow, the man apologized. "Forgive me, but there is an Inspector Thomas Levegue at the door. He is most insistent upon speaking with Mademoiselle Vallombrosa."

Rosalinda froze. She had been so caught up in the whirlwind romance that she got distracted from the reason she had come here originally.

Albert Vallombrosa looked at his daughter. "Why would an Inspector of the law want to see you? Especially at this late hour."

"That reminds me. There was an officer with Rudolph standing outside when we arrived. We thought nothing of it at the time because of the security Charles uses sometimes," Dominic remarked.

Everyone looked at Rosalinda for an explanation. As she was about to answer, Inspector Levegue walked into the room. "What in the hell is going on?" he inquired loudly. "Tonight, Pierre Bellefeuille appeared at

your play, and now you are having a party?" He shook his head. "I will never under-stand the rich."

Shocked, everyone began talking at once. "Rosalinda!" her mother cried, "What is this man talking about?"

Under a barrage of questions, Rosalinda explained what had transpired at the playhouse. "After that, I needed to feel safe and found myself here," Rosalinda exclaimed, looking at Charles. She knew he was her harbor of refuge, no matter what.

Inspector Levegue made a sound of annoyance. "And yet knowing the danger, you throw a party the same night."

"It is a not a damn party," Charles snapped, "It is our wedding."

Levegue stared. "Your wedding?" He could not believe it. "When my man telephoned me to say you would be staying here, I did not imagine it would be permanent!"

"Where I stay should not matter! What matters is what you are doing to capture Pierre!" Rosalinda snapped. "Now, you may go, or you can stay. But you will not stand there and accuse me of some wrongdoing!"

Tossing his hands in the air, Levegue exclaimed, "Bah! Have your wedding. When that American arrives, he is welcome to see to your safety!" He stormed out of the room, leaving everyone speechless.

"Well," Patricia said, "I have witnessed many dramatic exits since my son became involved with theater, but that performance tops all of them." She looked at her future daughter-in-law. "What was he accusing you of?"

Rosalinda shook her head. "I have no idea what is going through his mind."

Charles shrugged. "It does not matter." He walked to Rosalinda, putting his arm around her waist. "It is a beautiful evening, and if you are agreeable, I wish to wed in the garden, next to the pool."

Smiling up at him, the inspector's rudeness forgotten Rosalinda told him, "I would like that very much."

Looking toward the door where his butler still hovered, Charles nodded. Without a word spoken, the man hurried away to make the arrangements.

Chapter Eleven

The night sky was clear, and the air was calm. As though requested by the goddess, Aphrodite herself, for this special night.

At the head of the garden opening sat a statue of Anchises. That caused Rosalinda to smile. In mythology, Anchises had been the mortal lover of Aphrodite, her goddess. Was it by design she and Charles were to be together?

The five-acre garden was breathtaking even by day, featuring a series of unique, flowing spaces that housed over a hundred species of flowers, shrubs, and foliage. Pebbled, grass-lined walkways connected each area. At the magnificent garden's center stood a natural archway covered in ivy and flowering vines, which served as a guide to the granite-made swimming pool. Tonight, hundreds of candles illuminated the area surrounding the pool, setting the scene for the ceremony.

Rosalinda's family stood flanking her right, and Charles' mother, butler, and other members of the staff were flanking his left.

Rudolph and the officer, whose name Rosalinda later found out was Kenneth, kept a watchful eye on the surrounding vicinity. This was not an easy task under the darkness of night. Luckily, Heath had located lighting equipment used on a movie set for one of Charles' earlier films to effectively illuminate the entire area.

An hour after the ceremony, the Vallombrosa clan bid their farewells. Rosalinda's mother and her sisters-in-law promised to go to Rosalind's home and arrange for some of her clothing and personal items to be sent to Charles' home. They also would inform her maid what had taken place this evening.

The priest made his exit. Officer Kenneth and Rudolph agreed to take a shift standing watch until more security would arrive. Charles had contacted the security company he used during filming to watch his home and keep an eye out for Bellefeuille. Because he was so well-liked, there would be plenty of men available to help keep his wife safe.

By now, it was almost five in the morning. As much as the newlywed couple wanted to consummate their marriage, the reality was, they were both exhausted. Each of them had been awake for well over twenty-one hours.

Taking Rosalinda's hand, Charles led his wife up the back staircase leading to the third-floor master bedroom. Once there, he took her in his arms and kissed her gently. "I love you, Rosalinda, more than you can possibly know. I still cannot believe this is all true. I am afraid I will wake up tomorrow only to find it was all a dream." He smiled against her lips, "A dream I find I cannot finish as I am exhausted."

She caressed his chest, slowly unbuttoned his shirt and slipped her hands inside. "But we can hold each other while we sleep. We will have forever to make love after we wake." She looked up at him and smiled sleepily. Never in her life had she declined sex, but had he wanted to perform the oldest dance in the world, she would have turned him down. It would not have been the best way to start their love life, but her eyes were gritty, and she needed sleep.

Sex was the farthest thing from her mind.

He walked her to the bed, reached down, and folded back the covers of the masterly crafted king-size canopy bed. The bed, crafted from Birchwood, with Cherry, Pecan, and Elm veneers had uniquely large twisted and shaped marble pilasters, with carved wooden leaves at each corner of the bed.

Oh, she would love this bed! There would be lots of seduction and lovemaking in this bed with Charles, every chance she got. But for now, all she wanted to do was lay down, close her eyes, and let sleep take her where it would.

They removed only their outer clothing and climbed into the bed that gave Rosalinda the impression she was resting on clouds.

Charles snuggled, spoon fashion, and a small smile crossed her lips as she said softly, "I should have admitted a long time ago that I loved you. I would have married you just to have this bed."

A chuckle rose from him, but she did not hear it. She was already fast asleep and dreaming of the future she would have with him.

At two in the afternoon, Charles woke. He was almost afraid to open his eyes; not wanting to discover last night had not happened. But when he felt brave enough to open them, he found a pair of catlike green eyes looking back at him.

His heart swelled.

"Good afternoon, dear heart," she said, leaning forward and kissing him on the lips.

He smiled back. How could he not? He had everything he had ever dreamed of. "Good afternoon." His eyes roamed her face. "Have you been watching me sleep?"

"Yes," she told him, unashamed. "It fascinates me; the difference in your appearance now that you shaved your head."

Self-conscious, he ran a hand over his smooth scalp. "Do you honestly like me bald?" He had a tough time excepting that. He figured women preferred men with hair.

In answer, she raised her hand up, touching his scalp. "Very much," she said, moving up slowly, trailing that same hand down his neck, then through the soft hair on his chest. Gently she pushed at him, commanding him without words to lie back, and as he did, she moved on top of him. Then seductively ran her hands through her waist-length raven-black hair before slowly reaching back, unfastening her bra.

His eyes went hot as he watched her free her breasts. When she leaned forward, offering him one, he raised himself up on his elbows. Leaning forward and stroked his tongue around her nipple before taking it entirely into his mouth, teasing, stroking, suckling. His desire flared, as did hers. Her head tilted back, and she moaned. Her hands reached up; held his head in place while he tilted his hips so that the full length of his erection could be felt between her legs.

He thought he heard a knock at his door but did not care.

The knock on the door sounded once more, this time louder than before.

He could have wept.

86

"What is it?!" he demanded, turning his head toward the offensive noise.

Rosalinda gave a frustrated groan.

"I do not wish to be disturbed until our guests begin arriving for our celebration!" Charles barked.

Obviously, he hadn't been commanding enough; the knock became pounding.

"Speak English, damn it! It's Cadman Benson!" came the reply. Though muffled because of being on the opposite side of the door, the voice demanded an answer. "You might as well get dressed and get out of bed because I'm not going away."

Damn the man for his implausible timing.

Rosalinda rolled away, laying on her back, and began hitting the mattress with her fist. "I believe I now hate that man."

Charles could not agree more, as he rolled out of bed and found his pants from last night. He couldn't help the resentment that threatened to rise and choke him. He knew for a fact the person standing on the other side of the door had been Rosalinda's lover. And it maddened him knowing that he had yet to bed his very own wife.

Pulling on his pants and quickly zipping the fly, he marched to the door. Reaching for the doorknob, he glanced back to assure himself Rosalinda had covered herself. Satisfied that she had, he threw open the door and growled in English, "What do you want?"

Cadman's hazel-colored eyes were full of mirth as he took in Charles' appearance. Then he glanced at the bed to see Rosalinda sitting up, holding a sheet to her chest to cover herself. "Gee, I'm happy to see you too. I hope I'm not interrupting anything."

Charles had the uncharacteristic desire to punch him in the face.

"Listen, I've been traveling for over twenty hours," Cadman said. "I was happy as a clam visiting Colten and Jacqueline, in North Dakota, when I received a call from my office, informing me Bellefeuille is at large. The first place I went after my plane landed was her home, only to discover her staff packing her belongings. I was informed the two of

you got hitched last night, and her things would be delivered here." He looked to the bed and felt remorse that she would no longer be available for an afternoon in bed. But he had always known, deep down in his gut, their relationship would have never been anything more than consensual sex.

With a sigh, Cadman said, "Congratulations, by the way."

Rosalinda inclined her head in acknowledgment of his good wishes.

"Then," Cadman continued, looking back at Charles, "I arrive here to discover your staff scurrying about in preparation for a party you are hosting tonight." He rolled his eyes. "Are both of you insane?"

"The party was already scheduled before Bellefeuille escaped!" Charles snarled. He owed this man no explanation.

"What difference does that make?" Cadman exclaimed, "Cancel the damn thing!"

Rosalinda sat up straight; narrowed her eyes. "Why should we? We want to celebrate our marriage." She gave Charles a warm smile. "It was too long in coming, and I want the world to know how happy I am."

Again, Cadman rolled his eyes. "Send out fucking announcements."

Rosalinda, holding the sheet securely in place, climbed from the bed and moved toward the door. "Do not be a bore."

He couldn't help the lust that seeing her practically nude caused, so he focused on Charles's face instead. "I don't think it's safe."

"I have hired many guards. They should arrive soon, if they have not already," Charles informed the American agent.

"Cadman," Rosalinda's voice brought his eyes back to her, "I will be careful, I promise. I will be at Charles's side the whole night. You will be there. I feel confident in your ability to keep me safe."

He hissed. "Damn it, Rosalinda. Must you be so stubborn!"

She sulked, and he knew a lost cause when he saw it.

His eyes raked down her slender body before he knew their intent. "Put some clothes on, both of you. We'll talk about this downstairs." He turned to go, then stopped and looked over his shoulder. "Five minutes

is all the time I'll give you to get down there, or I will come back up here."

Rosalinda pouted. "I would like a shower before…,"

Cadman turned back. "Oh no, you don't. I know you well enough. A shower isn't the only thing on your mind. So, five minutes is all I'm allowing you. We only have a couple of hours to make sure security is organized before this place is overrun with guests. I suggest you take me seriously and get moving." He strolled away without a backward glance, almost whistling a tune. He could have allowed them more time. But he was sleep-deprived and thought it was great fun to deprive them of something too.

Rosalinda reached around Charles and slammed the door shut. "Have I mentioned I hate that man?"

"That makes two of us," her husband declared.

Stomping across the room, she picked up the dress she had worn last night from the floor where it had landed before she climbed into bed. It was a wrinkled mess, yet the only thing she had to wear until her other clothing arrived from home. She could not remember ever wearing the same thing twice in a row, let alone something that looked as though the house pets had spent the night on it.

Walking to the phone near his bed, which connected to a telephone in the kitchen, Charles picked it up and let it ring. It was answered by one of the staff, and he inquired, "Have any of my wife's belongings arrived? More precisely, clothing. If not, please see if any of the staff has something she can borrow for a short time." He glanced at his beautiful wife; he felt like the luckiest man in the world regardless that they could not consummate the marriage, yet.

It was fifteen minutes before the newlywed couple made their way down to the first floor and found Cadman waiting for them in Charles's office. Cadman had made himself comfortable behind the hand-carved medieval desk and was on the telephone speaking with someone on the other line. He glanced up when the couple entered the room. He assumed Rosalinda's clothing must have been delivered because that baby

blue dress she had on fit her as though it had been made especially for her.

Cadman motioned for the pair to have a seat in the chairs in front of the desk. He wrapped the conversation up quickly and set the receiver down. With a scowl, he looked up at the couple. "Your Inspector Levegue is a pain in the ass." He waved his comment away. "That's who I was speaking too, but it doesn't matter. He is as frustrated as I am with Bellefeuille and his ability to get out of prison with no one seeing anything." He leaned back in the desk chair, regarded the couple. Admittedly, they made a striking pair, and he knew Rosalinda would be incredibly happy with the man.

It was a bittersweet moment for him.

He rose, moved around the desk, and settled a hip on the corner. "Alright," he said. "Let's discuss the rules for tonight. Stay close to Charles, Rosalinda, and I'll relax a little. I'll also be nearby." He offered a slim possibility: "Pierre might not even be in Paris; he might have been satisfied just scaring you half to death." But Cadman dismissed the idea instantly. A mere scare wouldn't settle the score for Rosalinda's small part in helping Jacqueline elude him.

He shook his head, resigned. "Fine. I suppose I can't expect you to lock yourselves away until we find him. You have a life to live too. But we will take extra precautions. So, here is the plan," he told them, then walked them through the strategy for the night, hoping the measures would prove unnecessary.

Chapter Twelve

The staff was well prepared and ahead of schedule, waiting for the guests to arrive for the celebration party. They had outdone themselves and more than earned their wages. There would be a hefty bonus for all they accomplished on this day. Not only had they prepared the 16th-century château for the party but had also efficiently and quickly put away Rosalinda's personal items. No one would ever suspect Rosalinda's staff had delivered her belongings only a few short hours ago.

As the guests arrived, they were treated to buffet tables loaded with a variety of hors d'oeuvres that included fruit skewers, a variety of cheese trays, Bloody Mary shrimp, and prosciutto-wrapped pears with Blue Cheese. Waiters weaved around the crowd with trays loaded with cocktails made from gin, brandy, vodka, whiskey, and wines made by famous vineyards from around the world. It was becoming apparent that the news of Charles and Rosalinda's marriage had spread throughout Paris. The number of guests seemed to have doubled from the expected one hundred invited. Everyone, from government officials to those famous in the movie industry, came, regardless of having been invited or not.

As the guest list increased in number, the Chef de Cuisine was in his kitchen, losing his mind. He had meticulously planned his main course, which included Lyon-Style Chicken with vinegar sauce, Marseilles style Shrimp, and Duck l'Orange, for one hundred people, not two hundred and fifty!

He would be the laughingstock of the cooking community if he ran out of food!

As he began barking out orders to his sous-chefs and the army of kitchen staff, in walked Aimée-Louise. She had not meant to enter the kitchen, but the chateau was so vast, she got lost after using the powder room. She watched the chaotic scene unfold in front of her and could not help but noticed the panic in Chef Le Corre's voice. This was

contrary to the organized and streamlined kitchen that had impressed her when she first met him.

Her heart went out to him. Despite her mother's instructions not to dally in the powder room, she was not in a rush to return to the conniving woman. Perhaps that was why she stepped forward and inquired, "My dear sir, what has happened? What is wrong?"

"T'occupe! I cannot feed everyone! I do not have enough!" He hollered, not knowing what to do to feed so many. Suddenly, he felt the blood rush to his face in embarrassment as he realized he was, in fact, shouting at a guest of Mr. Lafayette. "Forgive me, Mademoiselle Fontaine." As he inclined his head in apology. Feeling that if the shortage of food did not get him fired, yelling at the woman surely would.

She waved the apology away as she stepped forward, her eyes scanning the Duck L'Orange as she went. Duck never had enough meat on the bone for two people on a good day, but they could make it into something else that would be tasteful and feed an army. "You could make it into a fettuccine dish."

His eyes almost bulged out of his head at the very idea, and he forgot, again, he was speaking to a guest, "Are you mad? Make a fettuccine with my duck!?"

Aimée-Louise ignored his indignant rant. "Allow me to make a small portion for you to taste! You will not be sorry, and what do you have to lose but an ounce of duck and some flour and egg for the noodles." She gazed at him. "You make your noodles by hand, don't you?"

He huffed. "Of course! There is no other way to cook!" She had better not have been suggesting he served pre-made pasta.

Without waiting for his approval, she grabbed an apron from a hook and immediately put it on, moving straight for the duck. She requested the necessary ingredients and mixing bowls as she picked up a knife and began cutting the cooked meat. Quickly mixing the dough, she ran it through the press and cut the pieces perfectly for her dish. Aimée-Louise was in her element; she loved to cook, but her mother forbade it, declaring it a common chore only fit for the lower class.

She had never seen eye-to-eye with her mother on that bizarre way of thinking, and she had disagreed with her on so many things over the years. Yet, she was always afraid to question or rebel, knowing the consequences would be too steep. Her mother was not a nice person on her best day, and when Lilith found out what part her daughter had played in helping Charles win Rosalinda's heart, there would be hell to pay. But for the first time in her life, Aimée-Louise had rebelled because she had recognized a lost cause when she saw one.

The staff momentarily ceased their activity, all eyes watching as the woman worked. The staff, in awe of the fact that Chef Le Corre allowed her to do so. He was normally very protective of his kitchen and equipment.

Le Corre scowled at the thought of his savory duck being added to a white sauce, though he admired her flawless execution of the dish she was preparing.

She plated the single portion, picked up a fork, and held it to his mouth. "Try it," she encouraged.

Hesitantly, he opened his mouth as Aimée-Louise slipped the fork past his lips. When the flavors touched his tongue, he tasted heaven. He had not thought it would be possible to merge duck and fettuccine, but the flavors, oh how they blended!

He stared at her and exclaimed, "Mon Dieu!" He began barking out orders for his sous chef to convert the duck into the savory dish. "Do it exactly the way she did it!" And the staff started hustling once more.

He looked at her once again, then blurted, "Marry me!"

She laughed gaily, knowing he was not serious. It had felt wonderful to produce a dish from scratch.

"May I create a dessert?" she asked with a plea in her voice, her eyes lit with excitement.

After the masterpiece she created from his duck, how could he refuse? At his nod, she began gathering ingredients and asking for any she did not see immediately. She became so lost in her art; she forgot the time; she did not notice when her mother appeared in the kitchen. Lilith

93

shouted her name so loudly, she jerked back from the counter, dropping the eggs on the ground.

Chef Le Corre watched, appalled, as Aimée-Louise suddenly transformed from a confident woman in command to a beaten-down animal, now cowering in anticipation of a strike from her master.

Lilith rushed forward, grabbed hold of the soiled apron her daughter wore. "You foolish girl!" she shrieked as she violently ripped at the apron. "What are you doing in the kitchen, working!?" The words came out sounding vile, as though the sight of her daughter cooking was the most repulsive thing she had ever encountered.

Stepping forward, Le Corre placed himself between mother and daughter. "Madam, stop! She has done nothing wrong!"

Lilith snarled at the man. "Who are you to speak to me?!" she exclaimed. "You are nothing more than a cook and should know your place!" She grabbed her daughter's hand, pulling. "Come with me this instant before people see you! This is highly improper! You are supposed to be mingling with the guests!"

Years of abuse had Aimée-Louise following along like a well-trained puppy. Nothing was said between the two of them as Lilith pulled her through doorways leading away from the party guests in the house and out into the garden. She moved quickly to a path leading to an unlit gazebo where no one would hear, or more importantly, be a witness to what she might do.

At the center of the gazebo, Lilith stopped, spun around, and slapped her daughter. "You foolish, foolish girl! Why are you so stupid? Charles Lafayette fell right into our hands, and you blundered that! You couldn't find a way to make him fall in love with you! My God! All of this," she used her hands to indicate the property surrounding them, "could have been yours!"

Holding her cheek, stinging from the slap, Aimée-Louise sobbed out, "I cannot possibly make any man fall in love with me! I can't even please my own mother!" She finished with a whisper. She had never dared to talk back to the woman, but tonight she had enough of her scheming ways. "Charles has always loved Rosalinda! He never had

eyes for anyone other than her, I could never compete for his affection. The best I would have gotten was to be a companion for him!" She smiled. "I am happy they wed!" she declared. "They belong together. Look around you! Obviously, all of France knows it to be true! I am not sorry for the part I played in helping Charles win the woman of his dreams!"

Lilith's face twisted with rage. "You did what?!"

She raised her hand to strike her daughter again; knowing if she had the strength, she would beat the girl to death. She had always thought of her daughter as worthless.

Aimée-Louise sensed her mother was about to do more than slap her, and she backed up. "Never again," she told her. "I am through with you! All you have ever done was force me to help you in your schemes, but no more!"

Tears streamed down Aimée-Louise's face as the truth finally crystallized: her mother would never love her. They had never gotten along, and she should have walked away years ago. But her mother's constant, intimidating threats bred a paralyzing fear, making her believe she could never survive on her own—not without the woman who had given her birth.

It was far past the time she stood up to her mother. The only time the woman would speak to her daughter was when she was grooming her to gain favor of a rich man, one that she could use to climb the social latter.

Turning away, she ran, not knowing where she would go. But what she did know was it needed to be somewhere her mother could not find with her.

Surprised to discover that her useless daughter had a backbone, Lilith watched as the darkness swallowed Aimée-Louise. Stunned and enraged that her daughter never understood the importance of marrying a rich man.

Hearing the roll of a small rock behind her, Lilith spun around in panic. The thought of someone having witnessed her confrontation with her daughter sent feelings of anger and apprehension throughout her body.

Looking toward the direction of the sound, she squinted. The glare of party lights mixing with the darkness made it difficult to see. Finally, her eyes caught sight of a figure that appeared to detach from a nearby tree. She was mesmerized by what looked like an angel, slowly walking toward her. As she felt the hair on the back of her neck start to rise, she was certain, if this figure before her was an angel, it was a fallen one. Into her view stepped a man. She could see him clearly now. His face was godlike, but his smile did not put her at ease.

"A pity," his voice soothing as he stepped onto the gazebo. "It is a pity your daughter does not understand what you so obviously wanted for her. Perhaps I can help." He gave an old-world bow. "I believe you wanted your daughter to marry Charles. Unfortunately, he is now bound to Rosalinda. What if his new wife was no longer in the picture? Of course, Charles would require comforting in his time of grief." His was voice was calm yet mischievous. "Someone to console him… perhaps someone he could fall in love with; grow old with?"

Lilith's eyes grew with calculating excitement, wondering if Satan himself had turned into flesh. That would explain the man's ability to be so hypnotizing. She now understood why Eve was so easily tempted in the Garden when she ate the fruit.

Lilith did not care who he was. He was offering her a means to resurrect her devilish scheme once again, and she had no qualms in excepting. She would do whatever was necessary to secure her place in society. "What do you wish for me to do?"

Pierre's smile was sly and devious as he answered her question.

Together they plotted a plan against the newlyweds. It wouldn't be long now, and he would execute his revenge.

Chapter Thirteen

Weaving through the crowd, Cadman realized he was actually enjoying himself, despite his earlier apprehension. He should be accustomed to rubbing shoulders with movie stars by now, but the experience still boggled his mind. He felt especially impressed because tonight, he'd held a conversation with actress Simone Signoret. Her sensual features and earthy nature greatly appealed to him; he had watched her latest film, The Sleeping Car Murders, with riveting attention. The film detailed a group traveling overnight from Marseilles to Paris by train, only to discover a dead body upon reaching their destination.

Cadman moved from room to room, watching for anything suspicious. He ignored one couple passionately kissing behind a pillar as he monitored the honored couple interacting with their well-wishers. He had never seen Rosalinda look happier, or more beautiful, than she did tonight. He wondered what had occurred to awaken her heart and finally accept Charles's love. Whatever it was, it had transformed her from being reserved with Charles to being utterly captivated by him. From afar, Cadman watched her hold Charles's hand, stroke his sleeve, and occasionally pull his head down for a heated kiss—each one met with cheering approval from the growing crowd.

Charles was one lucky son-of-a-bitch, Cadman thought to himself with a bit of envy. He would miss their sexual encounters. Rosalinda was not a woman to have affairs once she surrendered herself to a man. And it was obvious she was dedicated to Charles. It showed on her face, and with every look, she gave the man.

As Cadman continued to survey the room, he spotted Inspector Levegue loitering next to the unlit fireplace in the living room area. The man was not trying to pretend he was happy to be there. Having only met the man a few hours earlier and a few phone calls prior to his arrival, he had not yet determined how well he like the man.

Levegue 's displeasure was not his concern.

Turning in the inspector's direction, Cadman weaved his way through the horde of guests, dodging one partygoer who apparently had too much to drink. As Cadman approached Levegue, the man scowled.

"Quite the turnout," Cadman said, raising his voice a bit. Although the live band was staged outside, the octave level of the music carried well enough back into the room. The patio doors were left open to allow guests to move freely between the gardens and the house.

As a waiter whisked by Cadman quickly grabbed a glass from the tray as the man passed by him.

"You should not be drinking!" The French policeman snarled. "We should be alert. I dislike all these people being here."

Cadman doubted the man liked anyone being anywhere. "I'm not drinking, I'm blending in. At least with a drink in my hand, I give the appearance that I belong here. That stick up your ass makes you look out of place as hell." He gave him a mock toast. "Lighten up. I don't agree with them throwing this huge party either, but they are, so we might as well make the best of it while keeping an eye out."

"Baah," Levegue sniffed.

With a shrug, Cadman set the glass down on the mantle. "Do you have any leads yet?"

Doing a quick scan of the area before answering, the Inspector nodded. "We have found one inmate who helped in the escape. He is not cooperating, but I have every confidence my people will draw information from him soon."

"I hope so. For everyone's sake." Cadman glancing out the patio doors assured himself he could still see Rosalinda. "Has your coroner been able to identify the woman pulled from the river?" Not an enjoyable conversation to be having at such an event, but this situation required him to know as much information as he could gather.

"Not yet, but he will do everything in his power to match the woman's dental records with any that are on file."

Cadman moved closer to the inspector; lowered his voice as he asked, "Was she raped?"

They knew Pierre Bellefeuille for his sick perversion of cutting woman while he forced himself upon them.

Levegue nodded.

Out of the corner of his eye, Cadman caught a flash of yellow pass by. Looking in that direction, he saw Aimée-Louise slide against the wall as she walked, attempting to reach the other side of the room. The women looked upset; her shoulders drooping, and her left hand covered her mouth. Her troubled appearance made him feel uneasy.

Cadman's head motioned in her direction. "Do you know anything about that one? I just met her myself tonight when she arrived with her mother. Charles informed me he had only met her a few weeks ago, and that he had formed a friendship with her, but nothing more. He made a vague comment about owing her for her help." He shook his head, "I have no idea what he had meant by that."

Levegue looked her way, shook his head. "It is impossible to investigate everyone in attendance here with such a small amount of time."

That was understandable, but Cadman was more curious about the woman and where she was going that he excused himself to follow her.

Moving through the crowd, Cadman made his way out of the living room to the smaller dining room, located just past the foyer. He entered a small sitting room that allowed him to stay far enough behind the woman and go unnoticed. The woman looked over her shoulder before entering the study and closed the door behind her. He moved just outside the door and listened for a few seconds. Using the noise from the music to his advantage, he slowly turned the knob and gently opened it. Thankfully, the hinges were well oiled and did not make a sound. If she were up to no good, he could catch her in the act.

She was standing at the window with her head bowed. Her shoulder-length blond hair falling in curls behind her. Her arms were wrapped around her waist, her shoulders shaking. It took him a moment to realize she was crying, and his stomach clenched. Why did women have to cry when they were upset? Why couldn't they just hit a wall or something to get their frustrations out?

He wanted to be a coward. In fact, his foot instinctively moved backward, as though it knew the best course of action would be to march back out the way it came.

Suddenly, she cried out in anguish, as if she were in physical pain. Before he could overthink the situation, he walked to stand behind her. "Is there anything I can do to help?"

Startled, she spun around, her baby blue eyes full of tears and overflowing down her cheeks. She opened her mouth as though to speak but shook her head instead.

"There now," Cadman said gently. "Things can't be all that bad." He looked around for tissues and found a box of them on the small writing desk. Pulling one out, he handed it to her but kept the box in his hand, expecting one would not be enough.

"I'm such an incompetent, worthless fool!" she cried as she blew her nose. She covered her face with both hands and continued sobbing into them.

Oh boy, he thought on a sigh. What did one say to a stranger to help ease their heartbreak? "Is there someone I could get for you? Your mother, perhaps?"

Well, that question sure as hell had been the wrong one; the woman's crying increased tenfold.

At a loss, he moved forward and took her in his arms. "I wish I knew what to say to help, but since I don't, how about I just hold you up while you let out whatever has you so upset." For a moment, he felt awkward holding this woman he didn't know. But as Cadman calmly spoke and gently stroked her hair, he began to relax, and so did she.

He stood, being the anchor she so desperately needed at that moment. After a long, unknown stretch of time, she finally drew a deep breath and let out a sigh of release. She separated from him slowly and took a seat in a chair.

"I'm sorry," she whispered, looking up at him. Her eyes widened at the sight of his tear-soaked shirt. Embarrassed by the splotches of tears and make-up covering his shirt, she gasped, "Your shirt! I am so sorry!"

Cadman glanced down at the wet mascara stains. His mouth curved upward just a bit. "Don't worry about it. I can easily buy a new one. If anyone asks, I will make up a funny story about a run-in with an unexpected rainstorm."

He moved forward and took the seat next to hers. "Do you wish to talk about it?"

"Your shirt?" She looked confused.

He blinked. "Would you like to talk about what has you so upset?" he clarified.

She looked away and sat silent for so long he figured the conversation ended. He almost gave up, wanting to get back to his surveillance of the newly wedded couple. But just as he was about to rise, she said, "According to my mother, I'm worthless."

Cadman settled back down and waited.

On a resigned sigh, Aimée-Louise continued. "My mother is a cruel monster who uses people to get what she wants. Ever since I can remember, she has used me as a pawn in her schemes for a better social standing. She forced me to believe I have no choice but to go along with her madness. I had no one to turn to. I am certain she killed my father. I have no way of knowing if that is true, but none the less, I never knew the man. He was never a part of my life, so I do not know what happened to him. I asked about him once. It took me five days to recover from the beating she gave me. I was only five years old at the time. After that, I learned not to ask my mother about him. Now, at twenty-five years old, my mother still makes me feel like that five-year-old little girl, cowering in the corner as she barks her demands at me."

Cadman's anger was hard to contain, but he managed to sit there and listen to the young woman because she needed a friend, and he was there.

"I became a very obedient child. She was pleased, at least, that I hadn't turned out ugly. As soon as I was old enough, she paraded me around to men."

His fists clenched into fists. He would personally beat the old hag if the answer to his question was yes. "She prostituted you out?"

Aimée-Louise looked away, but he'd seen the answer in her eyes before she turned her face from him.

His body shook with the need to hit something as he forced his voice to be gentle as he said, "Continue… but, I think you need to talk to someone professionally and who will not judge you for things your mother forced you to do."

Slowly she looked back at him and whispered, "What if I told you my mother had flown us all the way to Paris because we are wanted in the United States for duping older men and taking their money?"

He was not sure what he should say, so he kept quiet.

"By chance, we met Charles when we arrived here. You can imagine how thrilled my mother was about that. She studied everything about the man so I could, as she put it, woo him into my bed."

Cadman shook his head. "I would say she hadn't done her homework well enough. I don't doubt for a minute he enjoyed your company, but Charles would never have looked at you as he looked at Rosalinda. He only has eyes for her."

"But I tried!" she cried out. "At first, when we arrived here, I went forward with her plan because I felt it was the only thing I could do to please her, but by then I could tell he was in love with Rosalinda," Aimée-Louise paused as she stood-up and paced.

"And you knew the gig was up," Cadman finished for her.

She spun around. "Yes, but it is not like you are thinking. I stopped trying the night he invited me along to attend the play she headlines. Before the show I was looking at a picture of Rosalinda and Charles. I saw the glow of love in her eyes as she looked at him in that photo. I knew right then; I did not stand a chance to be with him as mother wanted. Instead, I went to Charles and confessed what I had seen in the picture, I even told him what my devious mother was up to. For once in my life, I wanted to do something for someone else, and Charles is a kind man who deserves happiness." She laughed pitifully. "Regardless of what my mother has forced me to do over the years; I am a romantic at heart. I told him if he agreed; I knew just how we might give Rosalinda a little push, to be honest with herself on how she really felt

about him. Oh boy, was I right! It only took her a few hours to move in, claim her man and seal it with a ring."

Cadman stood. "I assume your mother wasn't happy with the news."

Again, she laughed. "That, sir, is an understatement! I told her we should not come here tonight, but of course, she insisted. I am certain it was only to find someone new to sink her claws into." She sighed. "I am done with her games. I do not know how I will make it on my own with no money, but I am leaving her. I want no part of her world any longer."

"I can help you," he told her. As she stared at him, he could see the suspicion flash through her eyes. He could not blame her; she had heard enough empty promises to last a lifetime. "I'm being honest here. If you let me, I have connections with some powerful people. I do not expect, nor want, anything in return." Stepping forward, he held out his arms to embrace her. Whatever Aimée-Louise had been through, she wanted to make a new life for herself, and he would personally help her find the right path to her own dreams.

It only took a moment for her to lean in and accept the shelter of his arms. For the first time in her life, she felt hope for tomorrow.

Chapter Fourteen

Laughing, Rosalinda turned to Charles as the band began their version of La Nuit, a song made popular this year by Salvatore Adamo. Taking her in his arms, Charles began to lead his wife into a dance, slowly swaying and rotating in place. The crowd cheered as the couple leaned in and kissed.

Charles whispered in her ear his intensions for their passionate night together as man and wife. Rosalinda felt shivers run through her spine and anticipation course through her veins. She could not wait for when they could finally be alone to consummate their love at last.

"Where shall we go for our honeymoon?" he asked.

"North Dakota?" she teased, knowing he was thinking of someplace romantic, nothing like the area her best friend Jacqueline called home.

The disagreeable face he made was worth the joke. "Well," he told Rosalinda, clearing his throat, wanting to please his wife, he said, "If there is something to do there…"

The music continued to play in the background as they stopped dancing to continue talking. With a coy smile on her lips, Rosalinda teased, "We could take a riding tour into the Badlands. Jacqueline and her husband have a horse business there. I really do miss my friend; I so wish she could have been here for the wedding."

Horses? Though he had never been on a horse, he wasn't opposed to learning how to ride, as he found the creatures beautiful. He had always admired those who could ride, and their ability to become one with the horse. Charles could not help but laugh to himself; learning to become one with a horse was not quite what he imagined for his honeymoon with Rosalinda.

He sighed. "If that is where you wish to go, then we shall go." Where in the hell was North Dakota, anyway? America? He knew that much, but other than his visits to New York City, he had no reason to visit other places in the United States.

She threw her head back and laughed gaily. "I adore you!"

His brow raised in suspicion. "Were you pulling my leg?"

Nodding, she told him, "Actually, I wish to go to the Gulf of Naples in Italy and stay in Porto di ischia."

Looking toward the ceiling, his voice pitiful, he said, "You really had me looking forward to learning how to ride a horse."

"Lier," she bantered.

"Perhaps a little." Charles laughed. "But if Porto di ischia is what your heart really desires, I guess we can go there instead." Kissing her on the forehead, he added, "Maybe after Naples, we can travel to this North Dakota to visit your friend."

Squealing with delight, she did a small happy dance. "Have I told you how much I-"

Her declaration was cut off by someone from the crowd crying out, "Oh my God! I think she is having a heart attack!"

Charles turned toward the direction of the shouting. Grabbing Rosalinda's hand, he rushed forward to see what the commotion was about.

"Call for an ambulance!" Someone shouted.

"I'm a Doctor," they heard a voice shout through the sea of guests, "let me through!"

Chaos ensued as people raced to find a phone to call medical help, while others refused to lose their vantage point.

Charles pushed his way to the front of the crowd and saw a woman lying on the floor with the man claiming to be the doctor kneeling over her. Getting a better look at the woman, Charles saw it was Lilith lying on the floor, clutching her chest. She looked ashen, her body withering as she moaned, "My heart!" she cried. "Oh, my heart!"

"Will she be all right?" Charles asked, kneeling, trying to help although he had no idea what he could do.

The physician looked at him and snarled, "I will know nothing until I can get her transported from here."

Looking up, Charles laid eyes on one of the staff; ordered him to get the crowd back. Looking back to Lilith, he spoke, "You will be all right. Where is your daughter?" His eyes did a quick scan of the multitude of faces, but he did not see Aimée-Louise among them. Seeing his Butler, he told Heath, "Find Aimée-Louise." As Heath left to search for her daughter, Charles scanned the crowd once more.

He did not see Rosalinda.

His heart stopped cold. Leaping up, he shouted out her name.

Inspector Levegue fought his way through the crowd. In a panic, Charles grabbed his shirt and hauled him forward. "Have you seen Rosalinda?!" he demanded. When the Inspector shook his head, Charles shoved him back, crying out his wife's name. His voice rising in sheer panic, he yelled her name again and again.

The focus moved from the poor woman lying on the floor to their host as he moved anxiously through the crowd, asking everyone, "Have you seen Rosalinda?"

The Vallombrosa clan pushed through the crowd as Dominic shouted, "What is it? What is wrong?"

"I cannot find Rosalinda!" he exclaimed. "She was with me just seconds ago, but now I cannot find her!"

The Vallombrosa's searched, spreading out and calling out to Rosalinda. They feared the worst. If she was not with Charles, it could only mean that somehow Pierre must have taken her.

Aimée-Louise rushed from the house with Cadman close on her heels. She stopped and stared when she saw her mother lying on the ground.

Charles grabbed Cadman by his shirt. "Rosalinda! Where is Rosalinda?!"

Cadman felt a cold chill of fear run down his spine. He would not panic. He would remain calm because that was what he was trained to do, but his heart thumped with uneasiness. "We will find her," he promised and hoped it was the truth, and he felt the guilt rise deep within himself. He had sworn to protector her, but he'd allowed himself to become distracted for a few moments and now…

He could not, would not, think of what her disappearance meant.

Continuing to stare at her mother, Aimée-Louise witnessed the small smirk that crossed the woman's mouth. "Mother! What have you done?!"

Cadman spun, looked to Aimée-Louise. "What is it?"

Shaking with horror, she told him, "My mother is not having a heart attack!" She pointed down at her mother, "This… this… whatever it is, was meant as a distraction."

Charles, crazed and filled with rage and heartache, reached down and grabbed the old woman by the throat, oblivious to the audience witnessing him manhandle the old woman. He did not care. He wanted to kill her, even though the thought of doing so scared him. The idea of where Rosalinda could be at this very moment scared him more. "Where. Is. My. Wife?" He loudly spoke each word with precise English, so the woman could not claim she did not understand what he was asking.

Lilith only clasped her chest and moaned. "Oh, my heart! Why would you treat me like this when I am in so much pain?"

He wanted to strangle her. The only reason he did not was because Cadman and Levegue forcefully removed him from her.

With a cry of anguish, Charles pulled away and began frantically searching for his wife as he called out her name. Along with his staff and several guests, he searched the chateau from top to bottom: scrutinizing each room, no matter its size. Others joined the Vallombrosa family as they frantically combed the gardens.

A half an hour later, the authorities arrived and began their investigation. They questioned the guests one by one before they could leave. They asked everyone to give details of what they saw or heard during the party. Still, there were no answers to Rosalinda's whereabouts.

Suddenly, a cry was heard from somewhere in the vast garden. The authorities, along with Cadman Benson, Inspector Levegue, the Vallombrosa clan, and Charles, rushed to where the sound came from. A body was discovered lying in the foliage. Benson forcefully kept Charles back while Levegue moved in for a closer look. If it were

Rosalinda, it would not be good for Charles to see what may have been done to her.

"It is Rudolph Forshaw!" Inspector Levegue yelled from the bushes. "Get that doctor out here!" Rudolph lay unconscious, barely alive. The inspector yelled out, "He has been stabbed and is losing blood." Without thought, he placed his hands over the wound on the man's stomach as he shouted, "I need something to stop the blood!" He continued to apply pressure until help could arrive. Luckily, the inspector had insisted the doctor from the party stay at the chateau; in case Rosalinda was found, and she needed medical care.

Lilith no longer required medical care, but she would need a good lawyer. She was in custody and being driven to jail, where she would be questioned for her part in Rosalind's disappearance. They would deal with her, but for now, Rudolph Forshaw was close to death.

When the ambulance arrived, and they loaded Rudolph onto the stretcher, he moaned, "Rosalinda. Bell- Belle- Bellefeuille." as he drifted in and out of consciousness. Though his words were no louder than a faint whisper, Charles heard his words clearly in his ears. "Rosalinda. Bell- Belle," Rudolph muttered as he drifted back into the darkness.

With horror, Charles looked at Cadman; the grief and guilt was more than he could bear. He should not have gone forward with this celebration. It was his fault his wife was in the hands of a madman. "My God!" he cried out as he dropped to his knees, remorse engulfing his heart. "I had her hand in mine, and then she was gone."

Firmly, Cadman told Charles, "Let's go back to the house. You need to sit down, and I need to make some phone calls." He would never forgive himself if anything happened to Rosalinda because of his own lack of surveillance.

Charles did not think he had the will to move.

"God damn it, Charles!" Cadman snapped, "You need to pull it together right now! I need to put all my focus on finding her!" He grabbed Charles by the shoulders, looking him in the eye, "I will find her, Charles. That's a fucking promise."

The ambulance pulled away from the chateau with its sirens screaming into the night.

Charles looked at Cadman and swallowed the lump building in his throat. She was not dead. He had to believe that, or he would drown in despair. "You will find her," he choked, his voice too raw with emotion to speak clearly.

Cadman nodded, praying in his mind that she would be alive when he did.

Charles did his best to hold on to the hope Cadman was trying to give him as he turned and began walking. Forcing himself to put one foot in front of the other, he walked through the garden toward the seclusion of his home.

Once the Vallombrosa brothers made sure their wives and mother were safely escorted home, they found Cadman and Charles in the small study. The brothers promised their father they would stay and assist in the search for their sister.

Cadman walked back outside to where he had seen Aimée-Louise standing by the now-abandoned makeshift stage. She turned when she heard him approach, her eyes red from crying.

"I do not know what to say," she began. "I had no idea the witch would go to such lengths to get her way." She wrapped her arms around herself, looking for comfort from the evil her mother once again managed to be part of.

It had crossed his mind that she might have purposely distracted him so her mother could execute her charade. However, looking at Aimée-Louise now, who was clearly devastated by what had transpired, told him she'd had no part in Rosalinda's kidnapping.

He did not know what to say to her but offered, "If you would like, I could have someone go to your hotel and bring your things here."

She shook her head. "No, that is exactly what mother would want me to do. I will need to find a different place to stay."

"Aimée-Louise-" Cadman began, but she put up her hand to stop him.

"I am so tired of that name I want to scream! Mother insisted I use it when we escaped to France." She sighed. "Although I cannot remember the last when I used it, my given name is Cynthia. Cynthia Payton. I am from America, and I was born in Nebraska; I grew up moving from states to state whenever one of my mother's schemes caught up to us." She looked away, tears forming in her eyes once more. "I don't know who I am anymore," she whispered. Throwing her hands in the air and shaking her head, she sobbed, "Here I am, feeling sorry for my-self when your friend is missing, and my mother took part in the ab-duc-tion."

Cadman stepped closer and put his arms around her shoulders. He vowed to himself to make damn sure he did whatever it would take to help her find the road to self-discovery once this nightmare was over.

Chapter Fifteen

Rosalinda doubted she had ever been so cold in her life. Her body felt frozen, but she did not understand. Wasn't she home in bed? Surely, that was where she was, lying next to Charles, the love of her life.

Trying to move closer to him for his warmth, she became confused. Why wouldn't her body respond? She tried to move her arms down to her sides, but they seemed held above her head, and her legs-they too felt as though they were at an odd angle and bound.

Reality came rushing in; she opened her eyes to see Pierre Bellefeuille looming above her, excitement and lust burning in his eyes. She screamed out at the realization that she was naked; spread out like an offering hit her full force.

Rosalinda struggled to free herself from the ropes that held her, but they only seemed to tighten more with each pull. She could feel the blood running down her arms from each wrist.

He smiled. "There. That's better. I have been eager for you to wake up. I was afraid I had used too much ether when I whisked you away from your little celebration." He reached out a hand, touched her cheek, then slowly trailed a finger down her body, over her breast, down her stomach and lower still until he had reached her pubic bone. "When you did not stir when I fucked you the first time, I was very disappointed."

She froze.

Her strangled gasp was a gurgled cry as the truth of what he had done to her while she was unaware brought new horror.

"Come now, Rosalinda," he laughed, reaching a hand to a tray next to him he picked up a razor blade, "You have had countless lovers over the years, one more man riding you should not make any difference in the world."

"Please," she whispered in despair, knowing begging would not stop him from whatever he intended to do, but she needed to try something to have this madman let her go.

He chuckled. "Do not worry, my dear, I'll be ready to do it again soon. I am already growing hard." He took the razor blade, and in one quick movement, he used it to slice her skin from breastbone to vulva. The cut was not deep enough to touch a vital organ, but it would leave a scar if she lived through the day.

She cried out, withered, and whimpered.

"There now," he said, and looked her in the eyes. "I have spent three years in prison thinking about what I would do to you when I got out. You should have never helped my dear stepsister escape me." He ran his fingers through the blood, spreading it over her breasts before he leaned down and sucked on a nipple. He moaned as her blood became a coppery taste on his tongue.

She bucked, and he slapped her across the face hard enough for her to see stars dance. She had a fleeting moment to wonder if he had broken her jaw because the pain was excruciating. Her eyes filled with tears, both because of the pain and the helplessness she felt.

"Don't you dare deny me anything, Rosalinda! You are an actress, so act. I am your master, and you will obey." He moved between her legs and in one hard push, entered her, heedless to her cries for him to stop.

Chapter Sixteen

No one at the chateau slept that evening. Inspector Levegue left for the police headquarters at some time during the early morning hours to update himself on the interrogation of the inmate who confessed to knowing about Bellefeuille's escape. Cadman escorted Cynthia Payton to the hotel she had shared with her mother to retrieve her belongings and then took her to a secure hotel. Her mother would be in jail for a long time to come, but he did not want to take any chances regarding her safety, or any deals her mother made with Bellefeuille before faking her heart attack. The Vallombrosa brothers and their father Albert stayed with Charles, knowing they all needed each other for support. As the hours ticked by, none of them wanted to give up hope, but each of them, deep in their gut, feared the worst.

Charles stood by a window, eyes gritty, staring out the window at the approaching dawn light. The anguish and guilt continued to wash over him. His knees felt weak, but he forced himself to bear it. He needed to be strong until they found Rosalinda. He refused to focus on what Pierre might be doing to Rosalinda, or he would go insane. Instead, he forced himself to think of what he could do for her once he had her back.

He would not consider the fact she could be dead.

Sensing someone behind him, he turned. Dominic stood there, looking shattered. Neither man spoke. They had said it all before. No one was to blame, except Bellefeuille.

Everyone jumped as the ninety-nine-inch-tall grandfather floor clock, with its Windsor Cherry finish, loudly began to bong, announcing another hour had passed without news. Eight o'clock in the morning and all was not well.

Seven hours had passed since Bellefeuille had abducted Rosalinda, and with each passing minute, despair rose higher.

Cadman stopped by the police station to speak with Levegue for any information he could get, but there was nothing new. No leads. No

witnesses. Not a goddamn clue. Disappointed to not have any new leads to share with the family, he drove back to the chateau.

As Cadman entered the study, the butler followed in behind him. Heath walked up to Charles and said, "Forgive me, sir." He looked uncomfortable for interrupting but, "One of the men working on the project on the East end has informed me there is a problem. As you know, demolition of the neighborhood begins this morning."

Charles stared at him. "Heath, why would you believe I cared about that at this time?" Fortunately, he was too tired to yell; otherwise, he probably would have shouted at the man for his unthoughtful assumption.

"Sir, the neighborhood is supposedly deserted; its residents all bought out, packed up, and moved out long ago. No one has been living there for months. The demolition company had been given the green light to proceed-"

"Heath!" Charles snapped. "I do not care!"

The butler turned to Cadman, a plea in his voice, and the knowledge his employer was too distraught to understand what he was trying to tell him. "Monsieur, Benson. You must listen to me! The demolition people saw a light in the basement of one of buildings to be eliminated today."

Benson waved a hand of dismissal. "Kids probably playing..." His voice trailed off as his mind comprehended what the butler was implying. Reaching out, he grabbed hold of Heath's arm. "Call Inspector Levegue, tell him to meet us there."

Albert Vallombrosa stood, sensing something was about to happen. "What is it?" His voice held excited hope.

Cadman looked around the room of grim faces. He knew the standard procedure demanded the families of victims be kept away from the crime scene. But there was no way in hell he would attempt to keep these people from coming with him. "We might have a good lead on where he is holding her." He looked at Charles, "Let's go. You'll have to direct me because I don't know Paris well enough to maneuver to where we must go."

"I'll drive," Charles told him and brushed past him at a fast run, headed to the garage.

* * *

Rosalinda was ready to die. There were no more tears. No more pleading. No emotion left to give. Pierre had used her in every way possible. Beaten her until her face was swollen so much, she doubted anyone would recognize her. She could not see out of her left eye and was not sure if he had blinded her, or if it were only swollen shut. The right eye was not much better, though if she wanted to open it, she could have.

There was no reason to open it. Rosalinda had no desire to see anything any longer.

He had broken her arm, which made her pass out once again from the pain.

Blood ran from the multitude of cuts he had inflicted over her body. He had used the razor to draw a line from just below the corner of her left eye in a 'C' pattern that ran along her jaw.

She heard him coming back, but she did not respond to the sound. There was no more fight left in her.

"Well, now, dear Rosalinda. We're coming to the end of the play."

All she could think was, "Thank God, he is going to kill me and release me from this nightmare."

He was half-way across the room when a shout rang out from above, and he reversed directions, heading to the door instead of to her.

"What is it!" he snapped to the man outside the door. The man, going by the name of Nolan, had aided in Pierre's escape and had stood guard the whole night. Now his face appeared in the doorway, "Someone is coming! It looks like a lot of cars, and I can hear sirens. If you do not want to go back to prison, we had better get the hell out of here."

"But I haven't finished!" Pierre screeched.

"There isn't time! You need to come right now!"

Anger coursed through him as he grabbed his pants; hurriedly put them on before adding a shirt and shoes. He glanced at his captive, unrecognizable now because of his handy work. "This is not supposed to be how

this story ends," he told her. "I was going to slowly cut out your tongue, then kill you." He rushed to the door. "But I will enjoy thinking about how long and painful your recovery will be. Perhaps one day we can do it again. Wouldn't that be fun?" Up the stairs he went, desperate to get away, and vowed he would never see the inside of a prison again.

It was time to travel to Cuba, he thought, as he climbed into the waiting car. He had always admired Fidel Castro. Maybe the dictator could use his rare talent for torture.

Nolan stepped on the gas pedal, just as the first vehicle turned the corner and headed their way. The car containing the fugitives jolted forward and into the night as the first car lurched to a stop in the very spot the escapees had vacated. More cars screeched to a halt behind them. The car with its sirens wailing and lights flashing continued forward, chasing the fleeing car.

Charles slammed on the brakes; exited the car as Cadman did the same, but as Charles rushed around the vehicle with the sole intent of finding Rosalinda, Cadman grabbed his arm; stopped him.

"Wait," Cadman said. "You need to stay here." God help him, he wanted to do the same, but it would do no good for Charles to see Rosalinda, if she was even here, in whatever condition she might be in.

Yanking his arm from Cadman's grasp, Charles snarled, "She is my wife!" He emphasized the words because, at that moment, he hated Cadman for whatever relationship he had had with the woman he loved.

Knowing it was Charles' helplessness lashing out, Cadman looked at Rosalinda's brothers, "Keep him here. All of you stay here." He looked at Albert, communicating with his eyes that whatever was waiting in that building should not be seen by any of them until he gave the okay.

Albert, being a father, wanted to deny Cadman, but deep down, he knew it was better all-around if they all stayed back. Looking at his sons, he said, "Do not let Charles enter the building; only Cadman goes in." He held up his hand to silence their protest. The only reason they obeyed him was out of respect for their father.

Cadman climbed the short steps leading up to the building's entrance. At the same time, he heard, rather than saw, the Vallombrosa brothers

restraining Charles. The man cursed Cadman Benson and the Vallom-brosa brothers to hell and back for keeping him out. But Cadman tuned it out, knowing the man's out of character behavior came from his need to get to his wife.

At the entrance of the building, he followed the glow coming from down the steps. Cautiously he descended, pulling out his M1911 pistol because he couldn't be sure there wasn't anyone else in the building that shouldn't be.

Debris crunched under his shoes as he stepped. He made it to the bottom of the stairs and slowly entered the space located there. He found it hard to believe the transformation of all the rubble he walked over upstairs to find what appeared to be a lavish apartment downstairs. He could have found something like it in the better parts of town. It was apparent someone had put the place together over a long time. Perhaps months.

And no one had noticed. How could that be?

He shook the question off. It had happened. How and why did not matter.

He carefully kept his eyes scanning the interior for any signs of another human.

When he came to the last room in the place, he looked in and froze in the doorway.

She was naked, tied standing in the middle of the room with her arms suspended above her, secured in place by a thick rope; the same type of rope that wrapped around her ankles and looped through U-bolts screwed into the floor. Her shoulder-length black hair was forward as her head dangled down and the blood-

He tried not to allow emotion to get in the way. He wanted to run forward, but he needed a level head.

She looked dead.

He swallowed the lump of sorrow that formed in his throat and told himself he couldn't be sure, so he moved forward, forcing one foot in front of the other until he reached her. Stopping in front of her, he

reached up, gently moved her hair away from her face so he could check for a pulse at her neck. What he saw, when her hair no longer obstructed his view, made him clamp down on his jaw so as not to curse at the sight of her dark swollen face.

"Rosalinda," the single word was a choked whisper, and he shook with the need to cry out his despair.

Her moan startled him.

Heart hammering with relief, he worked to cut her down. He had just freed her hands, supporting her weight when he heard the rush of feet clattering down the stairs.

He did not need to look up to know who had rushed through the door. He would not berate the Vallombrosa brothers for not staying away or keeping Charles out. Now that he knew Rosalinda was alive, he needed all the help he could get to keep her that way until she could be transported to the hospital. "We need an ambulance."

Now he glanced up, saw the horror and fear flash across Charles' face. "Charles, she is alive," Cadman told the man.

And when Charles came forward and knelt, reaching out to take his wife in his arms, Cadman gently moved away and let him hold her. He knew she would need him again and again over the weeks, months, and perhaps years. He knew it would take her time to heal from the physical pain, but the mental pain could take a lot longer to heal; if she lived past this minute, this hour, this day.

Silently Cadman moved to cut the ropes from her ankles, found a blanket to cover her with as he listened to Charles's soothing tones as he spoke to his love, assuring her she was safe now.

Theodore Vallombrosa ran from the room to make the call to summon an ambulance. His brothers and father watched helplessly from the doorway.

Dominic came forward, looked at his sister, and tried not to heave. "What can we do to help?"

Cadman examined Rosalinda's cuts and bruises. "I need water, bandages. Look for anything you can find in this goddamn place that can

help me clean and bandage the worst of these." He had some medical training. One did not work for the Secret Service without gaining some knowledge of how to apply a field dressing or two, and his past military history added to his experience.

Cadman doubted there was a needle and thread lying around, but he asked for the items, anyway. Some gashes would need stitches before the blood flow would stop, and to those, he told Leopold to apply pressure while he kept examining the starlet. "Be careful of her arm," he softly told Charles, "It's broken."

Charles nodded but continued to cradle his wife and stroke her hair.

She did not stir but lay there as though she were a corpse.

Cadman checked her pulse once more, assuring himself she still lived, and silently willed her to stay that way.

Inspector Levegue entered the room, looking grim. One look at him and Cadman knew Bellefeuille wasn't going back to prison today. But he would not comment about that just yet. Right here and now the focus was for Rosalinda alone.

"The ambulance is on its way," Levegue said.

Together the men worked at scrounging supplies, used them as Cadman instructed until the ambulance arrived to transported Rosalinda to the nearest hospital. Charles climbed into the back of the ambulance, refusing to leave his wife's side even for a moment.

Once the vehicle had pulled away, Cadman looked at Levegue. "One day, I'm going to get that son-of-a-bitch and kill him."

Levegue would not comment on that. No need to try to talk the man out of a vendetta when it was warranted. "Her bodyguard will live," he said instead. "I just got word that he pulled through surgery."

That, at least, was one life Bellefeuille hadn't taken.

THE
HEALING

Chapter Seventeen

Rosalinda was groggy, her body a lead weight. She drifted in and out of consciousness, mostly asleep and unaware of her surroundings. At times, faint voices would reach her, making everything feel like a dream. She tried to open her eyes, but they refused to obey. Through the haze in her head, she could catch snippets of conversation happening around her, but only isolated phrases came through.

"It is going to take a long time."

"She will need all of our support."

"Her body will heal."

"Most of the scars will fade over time."

She did not understand who they were talking about; it didn't matter; she took comfort in the drowsy dreamlike state and thought she might stay here forever.

Time passed. For how long she did not know. She felt a hand on her head, gently stroking her hair. She could hear a faint whisper in her ear, recognizing the voice, and was comforted to have Charles in the dream with her.

"We will begin to bring her out from the coma soon."

Coma? Who was in a coma?

She floated once more.

"Rosalinda. It is time to wake up."

That wasn't her mother's voice, and she did not want to wake up.

"You can do it, love. Open your eyes. I have missed seeing your beautiful green eyes. It has been too long."

Her mouth would not move. If it could have, she would have said no.

"Keep talking to her. The process can take a bit, especially because of the length of time she's been under."

"Rosalinda, there is a beautiful sunrise this morning. You do not want to miss it, love."

She sighed; obviously, he wasn't going away. Slowly she brought one eyelid up, then the other.

He was fuzzy at first, but once the vision cleared, she gave him a weak smile. Gazing into those copper-colored eyes she adored, she mumbled, her voice sounding like it was rubbing against sandpaper, "I love you, but I am going to take a nap." With that, she drifted off once again.

The room erupted into cheers. Charles sat on the edge of the bed, holding his wife's hand, as his tears flowed down his face. He did not care if a man wasn't supposed to cry. His emotions were raw.

Until now, no one had been certain she would ever wake up.

When she first arrived at the hospital, the doctors worked to get her stabilized and evaluate her injuries. They were uncertain if any of her head injuries caused trauma to the brain or how her body would react to the severity of her injuries. They felt the best course of action was to put her in a drug-induced coma. This option would protect her physically, and emotionally, during the healing process.

Over two hundred stitches covered her body, twenty-five of which were in her face. They had set her arm, the cast strapped to her chest. Coming out of the coma and recognizing her husband was the miracle everyone had hoped for.

Charles used the sleeve of his shirt to wipe away the tears before looking over his shoulder at the room filled with emotional family.

His mother looked on with tears in her eyes, as did Rosalinda's parents, and all her brothers filled every corner of the room, along with their wives. Absent from the joyous moment was Cadman Benson. He had been ordered to return to the United States, for whatever the reason only the American government knew.

With a tearful smile, Charles said, "She spoke!"

The doctor came forward and checked the sleeping woman's vitals. "That was an excellent sign that her mind is functioning properly. The next time she wakes up, ask her name. If she does not have difficulties with that, then we can solely concentrate on healing her body." He shuddered inwardly. He had never treated a victim of such a heinous crime and had feared the worst.

It would now be up to the woman to heal. Her acting ability had made him an instant fan when he witnessed her first play. He had seen her determination and her ability to transform herself night after night and film after film. Now he prayed she could do the same in her real life.

Rosalinda had a long road ahead of her. Her body would heal, but the trauma of being raped, beaten, and mutilated could damage the soul. There was no medicine in the world that could fix that. She would need to go at her own pace, taking back control of her emotions, step-by-step, and only when she felt ready. The process could take months, weeks, even years if her mind could not cope with what she had suffered.

From the time they found Rosalinda, Charles refused to leave her bedside. He held her hand and spoke to her as though they were deep in conversation together, making plans for their future. Even after the doctors told Charles that they were hopeful the worst was behind her, he did not want to leave her room. It took a lot of convincing to get Charles to agree to go home for some much-needed rest. Her family assured him they all would take turns staying vigilant by her side while he was away. She would never be alone.

When she awoke for the second time, Theodore was sitting in a chair by her bedside while Charles had left for a few hours. With a moan, she choked out the single word, "Water."

Quickly pouring a glass, he held it to her lips, allowing only a sip because he did not know if he were permitted to give her even that much. He smiled at her.

"Do you know your name," he gently asked.

She stared at him. "Are we playing a game?"

He shook his head. "But if you answer correctly, I might bring you ice cream later."

He had always known her one true craving, and so she said, "Rosalinda-" she hesitated, having almost said Vallombrosa. "Lafayette." She beamed. "I am a married woman! I am Rosalinda Marie Lafayette and do not forget it."

His eyes misted. "Never," he promised.

She tried to focus her eyes on the room. "Where is Charles-" her mind slowly panicked; she was not in Charles's bed or even in his house. "Theodore-" her eyes grew large as she scanned the sanitary room. "Where am I?!" Fear began to seize her.

"It is all right, Rose," it was hard to keep his voice calm, "You are safe. You are in the hospital. You are safe," he repeated.

"Why am I in the hospital? Did I have an accident? What happened?!" He watched her eyes change from crazed confusion to horror as the memories of why she was here hit her full force.

Her cry sounded as though she were in pain. Tears sprang from her eyes. She turned away in shame.

Theodore was at a loss. What words could he say to comfort, and the only thing he could think of was to reassure her. "You are safe." He moved closer, touched her arm, but she jerked at the touch, so he pulled back. "You are safe, Rose. No one will harm you."

Thank God the doctor walked into the room. With a glance, the man discerned the situation. "Good afternoon, Rosalinda," he stayed by the door. "My name is Doctor Brown. A boring name to be sure, but there you have it. May I have a look at you? It will only take a moment."

She turned her head to stare at him, eyes wide.

"I will be right here, Rose," her brother assured her. "Would you like for me to hold your hand?"

Slowly her eyes moved to his. Her nod was faint, but her brother saw it. He moved closer, reached out, and clasped the hand of the arm that wasn't damaged.

Doctor Brown moved forward, held a light to her eyes, checked her pulse, deemed her as well as could be expected under the circumstances.

"How, how long have I been here?"

The doctor hesitated for only a moment. "Three weeks."

She stared at him, shocked.

"Where is Charles?" She asked. Had he left her? Would he even want anything to do with her now that she was damaged? Oh, God! What he

must think of her! If he even realized everything that had been done to her, he would undoubtedly turn his back on her.

She couldn't breathe. She began to hyperventilate.

Charles couldn't have timed his arrival more perfectly had he directed it. He saw her distress and rushed forward. "Rosalinda, it is all right. I am here; love, I am here!" He reached out, stroked her head, cupped the side of her face that wasn't stitched and bandaged. "Look into my eyes, love." He kept his voice soothing, like softly falling rain. "Concentrate, Rosalinda. You are safe. You are safe." What more could he say? "You have gone through something traumatic, Rosalinda, but you are a survivor. You will make it through this." He gazed into her eyes as she controlled her breathing. "We will make it through this; together, you and I."

Her breathing slowed. With Charles as her anchor, she could push the horror away, and even if it was just for a moment, she held on to the comfort he brought. "You still love me?" she whispered in awe.

"I have always loved you, Rosalinda. Nothing will ever change that."

She had to believe that and knew she would need this man forever.

Chapter Eighteen

The days turned into weeks, but each day Rosalinda grew stronger. She did not like to be alone; ever fearful Pierre would come for her. Random sights or sounds would trigger a flashback to her time with Pierre, causing her to retreat to her bed and sob uncontrollably. Rudolph Forshaw, fully recovered from the knife wound, stood guard outside her room. He was happy to have been assigned the position; it helped ease the man's conscience that no one held him responsible for Pierre escaping with Rosalinda. He was a familiar face, and Rosalinda was pleased to see him doing so well. To ease her anxiety, he would stand in the hallway with the door closed to his back, only knocking to announce anyone wishing to enter her room.

At night Charles would sleep next to his wife on a roll-a-way bed the hospital staff brought to the room during the first week. She would sleep soundly, knowing he was there.

After weeks of steady progress, there was talk that Rosalinda would be strong enough to go home in a few days. When the doctor asked to speak to him in his office that morning, Charles assumed it was to finalize the arrangements for her discharge.

When the doctor arrived, he moved behind his desk and motioned for Charles to have a seat, then remained silent for what felt like an eternity.

"Well," Charles said, wondering why the man wasn't saying anything. "Were you going to talk, or are we to sit here looking at each other for the rest of the day?"

With a heavy sigh, Doctor Brown told him, "Charles, I have some news. I certainly do not want to be the one to tell you, but it is better you find out now rather than later."

Apprehension grew. "Then tell me."

"Rosalinda is pregnant."

"No," Charles cried out, feeling his heart squeeze tight. He reached up and rubbed his chest as though experiencing physical pain. The gut-

wrenching words hitting him like a bullet; he had no idea how to process the news.

Doctor Brown's eyes were steady as he asked, "Do you think you are the father? You had just been wed-"

Charles got up and began pacing the tiny office space.

He knew he had not fathered the child. What a laugh. He had been married to the woman he adored for almost three months now and never consummated the marriage. Nor did he know if he would ever have the chance because, although Rosalinda was healing and accepted his comforting arms, he did not know if they would ever have a sexual relationship.

He shook his head no, but quickly looked Doctor Brown in the eye, "As far as the world needs to know, I am that child's father." His tone warned of consequences if the dear doctor had any thought of saying otherwise.

God. The questions started flying through his head. Would he be able to carry through and love it? How would Rosalinda cope? He would not; could not make this decision for her, but if she chose to carry the child to term, would he be able to see it as belonging to him?

Would this set her emotions, as raw as they still were, back? Would her mind handle the shock?

"Do you understand me?" Charles was firm. "If she carries the child to term, if she is willing to be its mother, you will proceed as though the child is mine."

"Of course." The doctor nodded his head, feeling admiration for the man standing in front of him.

There was silence while Charles resumed his pacing. After a few minutes he turned back to the front of the desk, "Is she able to travel?"

"Yes. I was going to release her tomorrow. I believe it would be good for her to get out of the confines of this hospital and go home."

Charles shook his head. "No. Can she leave the country?"

"I believe she is strong enough to do so. What are you planning?"

127

"I will let you know once we have spoken to Rosalinda. She needs to be told as soon as possible." He was not anxious to shatter his wife more than she had already been.

"All right," the doctor agreed.

They walked down the long corridor as though they were about to face a firing squad; neither of them able to predict how the news would be received. As a precaution, Doctor Brown stopped at the nurse station and ordered a sedative to be readied. Rosalinda may or may not require it, but he thought it better to have the medication on hand instead of having to wait.

Alert and at his post, Rudolph Forshaw, watched the men walking toward him. He could tell by their grim expression something was wrong. "Sir?" he asked Charles with concern in his voice.

Charles shook his head. "Ignore what you might hear once we are inside," he told the man as he stopped next to Rudolph's right side. He leaned in and whispered, "Keep everyone back, unless the Doctor calls for one of the nurses, no one is to enter." The plea in his eyes told Rudolph, whatever was happening, it was not good.

He nodded in agreement as he turned and knocked on the door before announcing, "Mrs. Lafayette, your husband, and Doctor Brown are about to enter the room."

There was a moment of silence before she answered. "Thank you. Please let them in."

Once they were inside, Rudolph closed the door behind them softly. As he heard the door click shut Charles could not help but feel like the curtain just dropped to the floor. The next part of the play was about to begin; a part his wife never had a chance to prepare herself for.

She was sitting in the big uncomfortable chair that rested next to the window. The sunlight coming in bounced off her raven-black hair, making the dark blue highlights of her hair shimmer. The bandages on her face had been taken off and the swelling all but gone now. One could still make out the track-marks from the stitches removed earlier in the week. The right side of her face was smooth and radiant as ever. The scar on the left side of her face traveled from the corner of eye and ended

just below her chin. Time would tell how much the ugly scar would fade, if at all.

Charles walked to her side and bent down and kissed her, but not until after she offered her cheek to him. He was mindful of the trauma she endured and always waited for her to initiate touching or allow his kiss. He hoped someday it would be different, but for now, he was grateful he had her back.

Perhaps he was born to be a fool, forever living in fairy tales. Maybe he excelled in his film career because he was simply creating the life he wished he had.

Fantasies with happy ever after's.

Smiling up at him, she placed his hand on her cheek and rested it there. "I would very much like to go home." She glanced at her doctor. "May I go home? I am so tired of this place!"

Doctor Brown came forward. "I was thinking about letting you fly the coop soon, but before I do that… I… we," he glanced at Charles, "We have something to discuss with you."

"Oh?" She wasn't sure if she liked the way they were acting or the panicked feeling she was having. "Well then, out with it."

Charles grabbed one of the stools near the bed and sat in front of Rosalinda, taking both her hands in his and told her, "You are pregnant."

There was no reaction. Rosalinda looked at him as though he were crazy. "Charles, there is no way I can be pregnant." Once again, she glanced at the doctor then whispered for her husband's ears alone, "We have not…"

His eyes looked so warm, loving, and compassionate, staring back at hers as he said nothing.

"But." She swallowed loudly. "But." She began to shake as she realized what he was really saying. "No," she whispered, shaking her head in disbelief. "No!" She looked at the doctor. "Get rid of the thing! Oh, my God! Oh, my God!" How much more pain was she supposed to endure!?

"Rosalinda," Charles said her name softly, "You do not have to make any decision at this very moment."

"I want it gone!" she shrieked.

"The child is also a victim Rosalinda."

She sobbed. Her heart shattered. Never had she had to face a decision like this. She had always been careful in the past when she took a lover, never wanting to deal with an unwanted pregnancy. Now not only was this pregnancy not wanted, but it had also been fathered by a monster who would haunt her for the rest of her life. How could she be expected to raise it and be a mother to it when it would be a constant reminder of the nightmare she had lived through?

"I am not strong enough," she whispered between sobs.

He cupped her face, mindful of the still-healing scar, "I will be strong enough for both of us, Rosalinda."

How had this man become so strong? How could he possibly want her to carry this child and give birth to it, knowing it was another man's child? "How can we do this?" she cried. "How?"

"Together," he said. "We will do it together."

"It is not even your child! How can you be suggesting I give birth to it knowing it isn't yours?"

"Because, Rosalinda, I had someone who stood by my mother a long time ago and had he not been willing to love an unwanted child that came from violence, I would not be here today."

Gasping for air, she stared back at him, searching his eyes. She could see deep into his soul the honesty and determination of what he was telling her. How had she not known or even suspected he lived because his mother had not aborted him? She never thought to ask what his background was or how he had grown up. She had so much to learn about this man she loved beyond reason and who was willing to put himself aside solely for her. Could she not at least try to do something he asked of her, no matter how difficult it might be? "But every-one will know…,"

He shook his head. "You and I are the only ones who know we never consummated our marriage. As far as the world needs to know, we conceived the child on our wedding night."

She glanced at the doctor, who now seemed to have tears in his eyes. "He knows."

Doctor Brown cleared his throat. "I know you and Charles will have a baby if you allow it to live. As far as I am concerned, he fathered the child on your wedding night."

"You do not have to make this decision now," Charles told her. "You are still healing from something very traumatic and what I am asking of you will be the most difficult challenge you have ever faced. I want you to take some time before you make your choice. I believe you will find that easier someplace else. I want to take you away from here. I believe you would do well if you could spend time with Jacqueline."

Her eyes filled with tears and her heart flooded with more love than she ever thought possible for another. She needed to get away from Paris, at least for a while. If anyone could help her continue the healing process, it would be Jacqueline Fisher. She was more than a best friend; she too had been terrorized by Pierre. The man who was Jacqueline's husband had lost an eye trying to protect her.

Charles' willingness to take her to America spoke volumes to Rosalinda's heart. If he were willing to take her to a place so remote most Americans pretended it didn't exist, then she would have to consider everything he was asking; the welfare of the child she carried and their future as a family.

When she nodded, Charles smiled back, looked over his shoulder at the doctor, and said, "We will travel to North Dakota."

With a puzzled look, Doctor Brown asked, "Where exactly is that?"

Charles laughed. Having never been there himself, he assumed it was, "In the middle of nowhere, my friend."

Chapter Nineteen

Charles and Rosalinda started their trip to North Dakota a few days later aboard their private six-seat Learjet 23 and its two crew members. The couple waited until midnight to leave Paris to avoid any of her over-zealous fans or paparazzi trying to get pictures of Rosalinda just out of the hospital. Earlier in the day Charles asked the Vallombrosa family to leak to the press a statement; saying they were hopeful their daughter would be discharged from the hospital in a few more days. Rudolph continued to keep guard at the starlet's hospital room to avoid anyone finding out she was no longer there.

The entire flight from Paris to New York City took over ten hours, which included a quick stop to refuel. Once in New York City they planned to stay a few days at the home Charles kept there for those times he traveled there for his work. Rosalinda wanted to rest a few days before flying to North Dakota's capital city, where someone would pick them up at the airport there.

When they arrived in Bismarck, the small pyramid-shaped airport terminal had Charles marveling. For this being the Capital of the state, Bismarck did not offer any luxury for travelers. However, to the south of the current terminal, it looked as though a new and larger airport was being constructed.

A car was waiting for them once the plane stopped on the tarmac. Colten had asked his parents to pick up the Lafayette's from the airport and they were waving to the couple as they stood outside their vehicle waiting for their arrival.

Rosalinda was hesitant at first when she saw the older couple standing by their vehicle. She knew them and had met them several times since Jacqueline had wed their son. Although she had never been shy a day in her life, not knowing what their reaction would be to her appearance, her apprehensive caused her to reach out and grasp Charles' arm as he escorted her toward the vehicle.

Feeling his wife's grip on his arm begin to shake, he gently placed his hand over hers as they walked. "It is all right," his voice soothed. He hated to see how this once confident woman was now timid and doubting everything she had ever known. He desperately wished he could take all her pain and suffering and carry it for her.

He knew if ever the opportunity arose, he would kill Pierre without remorse.

Rosalinda glanced up at him as she forced herself to smile.

Colton's mother, Barbara Fisher, stepped forward to greet the couple and leaned in to kiss Rosalinda on her cheek. "I am so glad you could visit! I know Jacqueline can hardly wait to see you. My dear daughter-in-law defiantly has her hands full with the two older children but is really enjoying the new baby."

Rosalinda's eyes rounded. She had not heard that Jacqueline had given birth. "I- I did not know…," Her voice trailed off, and she swallowed a lump in her throat.

Barbra knew what had happened to Rosalinda and tried her best to reassure the Starlet that her not knowing was not because of the tragic event the woman had suffered "You know the mail service, dear, it takes forever for letters to travel from here to France. I'm sure the announcement is lost somewhere." She smiled. "Anyway," she continued, "It's a boy!"

Unconscious of the action, Rosalinda moved her hands over her still flat belly. For a second, she wondered if the child in her womb was a boy too.

Barbra had given birth to ten children and could recognize the signs of an expectant mother, but one look from her husband had her clamping her jaw shut no matter how much it pained her to do so. She loved talking about babies but knew her husband, Donald, would be the doctor overseeing Rosalinda's care while she was in North Dakota and would not risk her intuition over his doctor confidentiality oath.

"That is wonderful news," Charles said. "What did they name the child?"

At the question, Barbra wrinkled her face in discord. "Colten named him Hunter."

"That is a lovely name," Rosalinda began.

"Sundance." Barbra finished. "Hunter Sundance Fisher."

Rosalinda stared. "Umm" what could she say to that? But Barbra had named her youngest and last child Thaddeus Julius, so Colten wasn't the only one in the family to have given their child an unusual name. "It is memorable," she offered.

Barbra harrumphed. She hated the name, but loved her newest grandson.

Donald opened the trunk of the car to store the suitcases the couple would use for their stay in Bismarck. They would send the rest of their belongings to Medora via the train where Colten would retrieve them. The Lafayette's would stay in Bismarck for a few days for Rosalinda to rest from the long travel. Dr. Fischer could tell she was exhausted and knew there was more than the assault injuries draining her energy. Being a doctor, he had privileged information his wife did not, and until the starlet was ready to announce her pregnancy; he was keeping a tight lid on confirming his wife's suspicions. However, he assumed Charles was the father; Doctor Brown had not divulged the truth during their long-distance call when Donald was brought on board as Rosalinda's physician.

The drive from the airstrip south of town to the Fisher home, located just north of Bismarck, took less than ten minutes. As they passed the state capital building, Charles was intrigued by its presence: it was the only skyscraper in the entire city. Though smaller than the Eiffel Tower, it dominated the skyline. "That building seems out of place in this..." He paused, stopping himself from using the phrase cow town, despite how well it fit. Clearing his throat, he settled for, "It really stands out.".

The nineteen-story tower could not be ignored. It sat on the edge of the city, although there appeared to be some housing developments in progress to the north of where the building stood.

Obviously, this town was growing in population.

"The original State Capitol building," Donald said, "burned to the ground the morning of December 28, 1930." He turned left at a street and continued chatting. "I was twenty-five years old back then. I was just beginning my residency at Saint Alexius, which was the first hospital in the Dakota Territory." He made a turn onto Washington Street, heading north toward home. "When the fire broke out, the Secretary of State, Robert Byrne saved the original copy of the state's constitution, but he suffered cuts and burns on his hands while breaking a window to reach the document. Another state employee, Jennie Ulsrud, burned her hands when she attempted to save records in the North Dakota State Treasurer's office." They had been horrible burns. "The new capital, you see there, was built between 1931 and 1934, at the cost of $2 million-"

"Donald!" Barbra laughed, "He wasn't looking for a history lesson."

Blushing, the older man said, "Sorry. I get carried away sometimes."

His wife laughed. "His dad was the same way; a walking history book he was. Donald comes by it naturally."

Charles smiled, not sure what to say. As interesting as the knowledge had been Barbra was correct, he had not been looking for a history lesson.

Once the couple settled in the guest room, Rosalinda needed a nap. To ensure she would sleep soundly, Charles lay beside her. She did not have nightmares if she knew he was there.

The next day Dr. Fischer drove Charles and Rosalinda to his office at the Bismarck Hospital for her examination. She hesitated before entering the room. Although she knew this man and knew he would be professional and not hurt her in any way; she could feel her body start to tense. She had developed a crippling fear of men because of the unspeakable things Pierre had done to her.

"I will come with you if you would like," Charles offered.

I am safe; she told herself. I am safe here. He will not hurt me.

It wasn't an easy decision to make, but she had to try to attempt to get back to some form of normalcy. Taking a deep breath for courage, she shook her head no. "I will be all right," she told him, loving him and

hoped that one day she could fulfill the longing she would see in his eyes.

Once inside the room with Donald, she forced herself to stand behind a dressing curtain and remove her clothing for the exam.

She shook like a leaf as she put on the examination gown. She had to allow him to see her, to… touch her.

She closed her eyes and took a deep breath in and slowly let it back out; then another as anxiety waged war inside her head. She knew this man would never hurt her, but oh god how she wanted to run! Her mind wanted to close in on itself. To find a corner somewhere and hide there, where she would not have to face what had happened to her.

Finally, with determination, she squared her shoulders and forced herself to step out from behind the curtain.

Steady and gentle as only a man who had been a doctor for an exceptionally long time, Dr. Fischer finished the examination. Her lacerations were fading; the deepest one had been the slice down the middle of her chest. It was a miracle an artery had not been severed. He deemed the broken arm healed and took the cast off. He did not re-mark on the numerous scars marring her body, front to back. As far as scars went, the one on her face would be the least noticeable. She would probably never wear a bathing suit in public again, but everyday clothing would hide the others from prying eyes.

"You're healing very well, Rosalinda," he told her as she slipped back into her clothes.

"I need to ask you a question," she said before she lost her determination. She needed answers, and she knew she could trust him with this secret.

He sat behind his desk. "All right."

"Have you… Have you ever performed an abortion?"

Of all the questions he had thought she would ask; this was not one of them. It was hard to maintain an expressionless face, but as a doctor, he needed to keep his personal emotions and beliefs at bay, so he only said, "No," and left it at that.

136

She bit her lips nervously. "Have you been made aware I am currently.... Currently..." She couldn't say it. Tears welled up in her eyes, spilling down her cheeks.

He got up from his chair and came around his desk and sat on its edge. "I was told you are pregnant." Be cautious, he told himself. We're on tricky ground here. "You and Charles do not want the child?"

If possible, her sobs became unbearable. So much so he came out of doctor mode and became a comforter. Without thinking about the fact she might not accept his embrace; he wrapped his arms around her and allowed her to cry on his shoulder. And as the tears flowed, she poured out her soul, letting him know the truth. Letting him know who had fathered the child she carried.

After a time, she quieted. He said softly, "I can only imagine your turmoil. And yes, giving birth to a child forced upon you by a despicable human being would not be easy; keeping that child could be a constant reminder."

She pulled away, wrapped her arms around herself.

"May I ask- What has Charles said about the pregnancy?"

Wiping at her tears, she whispered, "He wishes for me to keep it. He... He wants to claim it as his."

Donald's respect for the man grew tenfold, and he said gently, "If Charles is willing to accept it as his, then perhaps you will find it in your heart to allow it to live. No, it won't be easy, and it is your decision. If you want to abort, I can have it done safely, and I most certainly will not judge you."

With a sigh, Rosalinda took a deep breath, let it out. "I do not know if I am strong enough."

"Rosalinda, you have already come so far after what has happened to you, and no one would expect you to make a decision like this quickly. You'll know the answer when the time comes."

She had to believe him. She needed to believe she would make the right choice for her, for Charles, for their future.

As the days passed, she contemplated what to do about the child she carried. Soon it was time for her and Charles to complete the rest of their journey to Medora.

With the encouragement of the Fishers, they borrowed Barbra's 1964 Pontiac Bonneville. With Charles behind the wheel, they headed west toward the empty plains.

Charles decided this must be the perfect place for anyone trying to disappear completely. He couldn't help but wonder, how did people manage to survive out here?

They stopped in the town of Glen Ullin, which was about fifty-four miles west of Bismarck, to have lunch at the local cafe and to stretch their legs. Charles could only guess the population wasn't more than a thousand souls.

Back on the road, Charles glanced at his wife and smiled. "Do you really like this wasteland?"

For the first time in an exceptionally long time, she laughed. A true round of happiness that had them both smiling together. The moment brought joy to Charles' heart. Perhaps this was not a place he would have chosen on his own, but he would walk through hell if it brought life back into her eyes.

"Yes. It is beautiful here. Soon you will enter the badlands, and oh my dear you could never imagine the majesty until you see it."

He held his skepticism at bay, but as the landscape started to change, he could see for himself the spectacular color display. The colors alternated from black coal to bright clays to red scoria, and his talented scouting eye could see a backdrop for a movie. Yes, he might see an appeal to this place, but only to visit, not to live.

He hoped to whatever god there might be that his wife would not want to remain here and would long for Paris as he did.

It was in a little less than an hour later when they arrived at the town of Medora; that is, if one really chose to call it a town.

Rosalinda looked out the window as Charles slowed the car at the edge of town. She told her husband softly, "My great grandfather's brother founded this town and named it after his wife."

Charles was intrigued. "I do not understand…,"

"His name was Antoine-Amédée-Marie-Vincent Manca Amat de Vallombrosa, Marquis de Morès et de Montemaggiore. He was an entrepreneur. Eighty-three years ago, he moved here and wanted to butcher cows and send the beef by rail to Chicago." She pointed toward a lone chimney that could be seen in the distance. "That chimney and a few cornerstones are all that remains of the slaughterhouse he had built to begin his dream." Her hand moved in a different direction to point out what appeared to be a large home resting at the top of the hill which overlooked the town. "The structure there was the hunting lodge and summer home Antoine had built for his family. My distant cousin Louis, Antoine and Medora's son, donated it to this state in 1936 on the condition it is maintained and opened to the public."

Charles could only marvel.

"There is more history here," Rosalinda said. "A United States President spent time here as a rancher when he was younger. This might be a small town, but its history is truly amazing."

"Perhaps there is a story to be told here," Charles said, and his mind wondered what the possibilities were of making a documentary of this place.

Rosalinda gave directions to Colten and Jacqueline's home, and soon they were following billboard signs that advertised an "Adventure of a Lifetime! Get to the heart of the Badlands on horseback today!"- They were soon pulling into the entrance of the Fisher spread.

Charles found himself genuinely impressed with the place. The main house, a three-story stone château, was situated on top of a hill overlooking the property and resembled the architecture he was used to in Paris. Seeing it, he felt such overwhelming relief he could have cried; he had truly assumed the Fishers lived in a shack.

As the car rolled to a stop in front of the home, they could see the front door open, and Jacqueline stepped out. There was a baby in her arms,

but she handed the bundle to another woman who followed her outside. Once her hands were free, she rushed toward the car as Rosalinda stepped out.

Arms enfolding around each other, they both wept with joy and sorrow, and Charles knew he had made the right decision bringing his wife here.

Chapter Twenty

The early morning hours were spent reliving childhood and public events across France. But the casual talk gave way to a somber reality as Rosalinda shared the night that changed everything, including the decision facing her about her pregnancy. Jacqueline listened, reliving her own trauma with Pierre. Though her encounter wasn't as hideous as Rosalinda's, she instantly recognized the depth of unspeakable terror her friend had endured. Jacqueline's heart ached, listening as Rosalinda confessed wanting to die that night, just to escape the pain, the shame, and the utter hopelessness of being violated. Without needing any words, Jacqueline held Rosalinda, offering a safe space to release everything she had bottled up inside.

In the morning, Colten, who allowed no one to see under the patch covering the eye and cheekbone that had been damaged when Pierre had viscously slammed a hand-sized rock into it, made the exception to the rule and uncovered it for Rosalinda to view.

"It took me a long time to adapt to having the use of only one eye," Colten told her, "When someone would come up on my left side, without me knowing, it would spook me sometimes." He looked at Rosalinda and said with passion, "You'll heal, Rosalinda. You can't allow Pierre to break your spirit any more than he has, and you'll be a hell of a lot stronger woman than you already are."

As the days and weeks moved forward, Rosalinda pondered Colten's declaration. She needed to move forward with her life. It would not be easy, but she could take it day by day and see what came next.

One day, while Jacqueline was away at the ranch's food hall, Rosalinda heard the baby begin to fuss after waking from his nap. She thought to call the housekeeper, who was busy in the garden, but paused. She listened quietly as the infant's cries turned to soft cooing. She then walked slowly toward the nursery doorway, feeling irresistibly drawn to the sound—a sweet melody she had never truly heard until now.

Rosalinda hesitated in the doorway.

Suddenly she heard a young voice from behind her say, "Pick him up."

When she turned around, she found three-year-old Donna Fisher look-ing up at her, innocently sucking on a lollipop she wasn't supposed to have. "If you don't, he's going to cry the house down. I can't do it 'cuz mama would have my head, and daddy would give me a good spank-ing." Her eyes took on a wide-eyed conspiracy look as she whispered, "I don't think spankings."

Relying on her acting ability, Rosalinda kept her face relaxed despite wanting to laugh. "I do not like them either, but sometimes they happen to little girls who take lollipops without permission."

Donna popped the treat out of her mouth and put it behind her back so quickly it was a blur. "What lollipop?"

The baby continued to wail. "Shouldn't you pick him up?"

Rosalinda refused to let the unsaid dare get the best of her. She marched to the crib, reached down, and lifted the baby, supporting his head and placing him in the crook of her arm. She had held plenty of infants over the years—her nieces, nephews, cousins, and countless ba-bies of fans who wanted a photo. She was always happy to indulge, but she never felt a special bond. Now, however, as she gazed down at baby Hunter, who was quiet and gazing back with deep brown eyes, she felt her heart suddenly melt..

"You have to support his head," came a new voice, Rosalinda looked up to see the Fisher's oldest child, ten-year-old Clinton, standing in the room. He looked nervous at seeing someone outside of the family hold-ing his baby brother.

Young Donna rolled her eyes. "She already is, silly."

Rosalinda glanced back and forth between the two children. She knew the immense happiness they brought her best friend, and how easily Jacqueline and Colton had overcome the challenges of a blended family. Though Clinton was Colton's son from his late first wife, Jacqueline loved the boy and treated him as her own. Rosalinda realized she herself loved both Fisher children with all her heart; did blood really matter? Was this why Charles was so willing to accept the baby growing inside her as his own? Because his love ran so deep that lineage was irrelevant?

And if that was true, what made the child in her womb any less innocent simply because his conception stemmed from violence? Charles had been right: the child Pierre placed inside her was just as much a victim as she was.

Glancing back down at baby Hunter, it startled her to see droplets of water on him and realized they were her own tears. "Oh!" she exclaimed, batting away the tears on her face, and then used a blanket to dry them from Hunter's. "I am sorry, little one," she smiled down at him.

Clinton shook his head as he wrinkled his nose. "Women are funny."

Donna, offended, told him, "We are not!"

"You're not a woman!" Clinton exclaimed.

Both kids, posturing like grizzly bears, ready to pounce on each other, and Donna threatening to pull her brother's hair out, frozen in place when they heard their mother say one word, "Don't."

Jacqueline continued into the room and said to her daughter, "I know what's behind your back, and we'll talk later." Smiling at Rosalinda she told her friend, "I figured Hunter was probably awake and wanting to be fed. Thank you for coming to his rescue." She did not remark on the moisture still clinging to Rosalinda's face but took Hunter from her arms and headed toward the bedroom where she could breastfeed in private.

Once Hunter was full once again, and his diaper changed, he was content to lay in his crib, watching the musical windup horse mobile hanging above the crib. Jacqueline found her friend outside standing on the wraparound porch, leaning with her arms crossed onto the rail, watching the activity of the ranch. Horses were coming back from a trail ride as others were being prepared and mounted for the next excursion. From the barn, they could see the temporary summer help moving wheelbarrows in and out to refresh the straw in the stables as others cared for the horses fresh off the trail.

As the women watched, they looked on in wonder as Charles strolled through the coral in a pair of blue jeans, a plaid shirt, cowboy boots, and a brown Stetson fixed atop of his head.

"That's some man you have, Rosalinda. I don't know if I know of anyone who loves a woman as much as he loves you."

As Rosalinda watched Charles cross the yard, a lump of emotion swelled in her throat, forcing her to blink back tears. She never imagined it was possible to be loved the way Charles loved her. She deeply regretted not acknowledging her true feelings sooner, because yes, she loved that man with all her heart. He was stronger than she would have thought possible for a man so openly desiring a woman. She often saw the longing in his beautiful eyes, but at night in bed, he simply held her, making her feel safe, and never asked for anything she wasn't ready to give.

Her throat was tight with emotion, but she managed to say, "Colten probably loves you as much as Charles loves me."

On a dreamy sigh, Jacqueline agreed. "But Charles, he has loved you forever. What caused you to finally wake up and smell the roses?"

On a laugh, Rosalinda confided. "Another woman."

Jacqueline's eyes bulged. "Charles, our Charles, was dating another woman?"

"Not really," Rosalinda shook her head. Charles had confessed recently to the gamble he had taken. His one last effort to win her affection, and Aimée-Louise's part in it. "Cadman told me the woman's real name is Cynthia, but I do not care. At the time, she had me convinced she and Charles were a couple. When I saw her wrapping herself around him...?" She paused, then shook her head. "It broke my heart. I believe I have always loved him, but the thought of losing him helped me to see how foolish I had been."

Rosalinda's eyes were fixated on Charles as she watched him stop to talk with Colten. She admired the way her husband filled out a pair of blue jeans. Who would have thought a man who usually dressed in the finest business suits money could buy could look that damn good in denim?

"I never knew a man could love a woman, truly love a woman, without sex being their main objective." She glanced at Jaqueline, shrugged her

shoulders, and smiled. "Your Colten is the exception. He would love you no matter what."

Jaqueline watched as her husband turned to his son and pointed toward the coral as he spoke to Clinton. The boy ran off to do whatever Colten had told him to. She would never tire of looking at her handsome cowboy.

"I do not know how to tell Charles how deeply I love him," Rosalinda continued. "He is so patient and good. I love him beyond words."

Then, seeing Clinton leading a horse toward where Charles stood, she gasped. When Charles began to mount the horse, her eyes bulged, and she exclaimed, "What is he doing?! He will kill himself!"

Patting her friend's arm and laughing, Jacqueline said, "He will be fine. He has been getting advice from Colten about horseback riding, and today he is going on a trail ride to get used to the saddle. The horses we use for the tourists are older and very gentle, and besides, Colten won't let anything happen to him." They watched Colten mount his own horse and begin to lead the horse Charles was riding toward the group of tourists anxiously waiting to experience areas of the Badlands one could only see from the navigated trails.

As the dozen or so riders faded from view, Rosalinda blurted, "I am going to keep the child!"

Startled by the sudden outburst, Jacqueline said, "What?"

"The baby. My baby. I am going to keep the baby." She would do it for Charles, and she knew that with the man she adored, she would be able to see the innocent child growing inside of her as a blessing and not a curse.

Rosalinda did not fool herself into thinking it would be easy to raise the child. But she was committed to Charles, and he overflowed with love.

Throwing her arms around her best friend, Jacqueline squealed with delight. "I am so happy! Perhaps Hunter and your baby will be the best of friends too."

Rosalinda hoped that would be true and hoped the excitement of her decision would last over the coming months.

"Jacqueline," she said, hesitant at first, but in her heart, she knew she was ready. And her husband deserved a wife in all ways. "I know things are very hectic at the ranch, but is there any way you could drive me to Dickinson?"

"Well, maybe. Is there something special you wanted to pick up?"

An uncharacteristic blush flooded the starlet's face. "I- I thought I would like to purchase a negligee."

On a laugh, Jacqueline said, "I don't care how busy we are. I'll make the arrangements with the staff, and then you and I, my dear friend, are heading into town to buy something that will knock your man's socks off!"

Chapter Twenty-One

Colten slowed his horse, maneuvering off the trail to let a group of tourists pass, and motioned for Clinton to take the lead. Colten couldn't have been prouder of all his ten-year-old son had achieved, especially his excellence with horses. Colten credited Jacqueline's gift for working with children who have mental and physical disabilities, which helped Clinton find effective ways to manage situations that once caused him anxiety. Working with the horses was also her idea, incorporated for therapeutic care and focus. This comprehensive approach worked so well that most people wouldn't even suspect he had autism. Jacqueline, who first came to the U.S. as a foreign exchange student to study learning disabilities, began working with Clinton shortly after she entered their lives.

Jacqueline told Colten early on that she wanted to homeschool Clinton and their future children, and Colten backed her completely. They constantly heard the criticism and unsolicited opinions about homeschooling. The primary concern people raised was that the children wouldn't get socialized. It was never about the curriculum, only about peer interaction. The sheer absurdity of this argument baffled Colten. Given the constant flow of people of all ages; staff during the winter and tourists in the summer, how much more socialized could they be? Furthermore, the children were expected to pitch in with necessary chores, proving that a little hard work was a crucial part of their education.

The horse Charles was riding was the last in line. As his horse neared Colten's mount, the former Secret Service agent reined in his own mount and set it to walk next to Charles as they continued following the group in front of them.

"You seem to be enjoying yourself," Colten remarked.

Charles's grin was ear-to-ear. "Absolutely!" he exclaimed. "This is a wonderful experience, and I hope to do it more often. I am sure I will not have any problem convincing my wife to visit at least once a year."

With a laugh, Colten told him, "You're a natural. Are you sure you have never ridden a horse before?"

"This is my first time, but I can honestly say, it will not be the last time. And the scenery! My God! More people need to visit this area! I understand one of your states local businessmen intends on turning the small town of Medora into a tourist attraction. I think he would be right to do so."

"Has your wife told you her connection with the town?"

Charles nodded. "Yes, she shared a little of her family's history with me, and I find the story fascinating."

"That it is," Colten said.

"Perhaps one day…," Charles paused, looked at the land. "Perhaps one day she will tell me more about it. I also believe that somehow, this land is helping her to heal." He had to hope that was true.

Colten reined in, stopped his horse, and Charles did the same. "She's getting better. It's going to take time."

"I know! I know it is, and each day she is becoming more like herself. It has done her good to be here where there are open spaces and nothing to trigger a memory of that horrific night! I do worry she may not want to return to Paris or ever want to take the stage again because she fears people will talk about it behind her back. She cannot see that she is still as beautiful as ever, and that scar on her face can be concealed with make-up. They cannot see the scars on her body when she has clothes on. That is something to be thankful for." He shook his head. "Acting is her life. The passion she has on film and on the stage comes forth like a bright light. She is the best leading lady I have ever cast in one of my movies."

Colten chuckled, "Not that you are biased, she being your wife and all."

Charles scowled. "She is famous worldwide. I am surprised no one has recognized her here."

With a laugh, Colten said, "She stays close to the house, but remember where you are. No one would think to look for a famous person here. It's," he used his fingers as quotation marks, "The end of the earth."

"But beautiful," Charles chuckled along with him.

They set their horses in forward motion once again.

"I do have an idea that might nudge her back onto the stage," Colten said. "In Medora, there's an amphitheater. Harold Schafer, the man restoring the town, bought the place, made some changes, and hired Al Sheehan productions to put on an outdoor variety show. There's a performance tonight. I can make arrangements with my staff, and we could take the ladies out for a night of entertainment. Who knows, seeing a live show might just give Rosalinda the acting itch again."

"I have not known you long, but has anyone ever told you how brilliant you are?"

"I think my wife told me that once, but I am not sure she would admit it." Colten smiled.

They talked about the upcoming night, and once they ended that subject, Charles said, "Colten, what you are doing here is marvelous, and if you allowed me to do so I would like to become an investor in this ranch."

Had Colten not been an experienced horseman, he would have fallen out of the saddle. "You want to invest?" He clarified; perhaps he had heard wrong. He did not need an investor; he was financially secure, but it never hurt to have the extra cash flow.

"A silent partner of course; you would continue to run this place in your own way because, after all, you seem to know what you are doing. But I like the idea of having something here people would enjoy as much as they do my movies."

"I'll think about it," Colten told him, and they continued the journey with only the creak of leather and hoof steps in the dirt breaking the silence.

Later that evening, as he watched his wife and Rosalinda preparing for the evening meal at the kitchen counter, Colten broached the subject of attending the night's production at the outdoor stadium.

Jacqueline whooped. "Oh my gosh, that would be so much fun!" Looking to see Rosalinda's reaction she saw the apprehension cross her friend's face. "You will love it!" she told her, "We must dress warmly because once the sun goes down, it gets chilly sitting there. A long sleeve shirt would be perfect." Knowing it would cover the scars on Rosalinda's arms if she was feeling anxious about going out for the first time. Without bringing up the scars she wanted to reassure her friend there would be no need to feel out of place, as everyone would be dressed in the same fashion for warmth.

"Umm…" Rosalinda's hand went to the scar on the left side of her face.

Charles stepped forward, gently stroking her arm, "Have you noticed how many women around here seem to wear their hair down and pulled to the side in a ponytail?" He looked at her with encouragement in his eyes. "I have always loved your beautiful hair and like it best when it is down."

Rosalinda narrowed her eyes. "So, you married me for my hair because you do not have any?"

Delighted with her spirited answer, Charles threw his head back and laughed.

"It will help the hours pass by before it's time for bed," Jacqueline said, giving her friend a look that had Colten raising an eyebrow. He knew that look. Something was in the wind, but Colten was smart enough not to ask out loud what his wife had in the making. The last time he'd done that, she accused him of ruining a birthday surprise for him, and yet all he had asked was why she had an innocent, "I know something you don't know" expression. He hadn't known about the party, but he sure learned to keep his mouth shut.

He did not like sleeping in a different room without her.

Rosalinda looked at Charles. She could see the excitement in his eyes and knew it was something he would enjoy. Jacqueline was right, it

would help fill the hours before she went through with the plans she had for Charles tonight. "Perhaps," she licked her lips before squaring her shoulders and flashing Charles a radiant smile. "Perhaps it will be enjoyable to discover if these Americans know anything about putting on a show."

Charles couldn't stop himself; he moved in and kissed her quickly, pulling back before she could sense the passion he held for her. He certainly didn't want to spook her, but he ached for her constantly. Every night, he lay next to her, holding her securely, always careful not to touch her in any way that might make her feel guilty or pressured. Because of his love, it was excruciating not to show her the full depth of his desire. But he had waited what felt like a lifetime just for her to realize she loved him; he would wait for her to be ready to desire him in bed, even if he knew that day might never come.

God help him.

"Oh!" Jacqueline said, clapping her hands together. "Wonderful! Let's go find something for you to wear," she told Rosalinda. "And we'll need to bring a few blankets in case it gets colder than we like…" she stopped, hit her forehead with the palm of her hand, and looked at Colten. "We drove into Dickinson earlier for a little shopping, and while we were in town, I stopped by the tractor supply and picked up those parts you wanted."

Colten, about to take a drink of coffee from his mug, gestured with it toward Charles. "Best woman living in North Dakota." He would have said the world, but with Rosalinda standing right there, that wouldn't seem right. "What else did you pick up?"

She tsked. "You just never mind, Colten Fisher."

Colten shook his head. Some days he was damned if he did and damned if he didn't.

An hour later, they left the ranch, having eaten a hasty supper to ensure they reached the outdoor theater before the show began. Driving through town, they turned onto the winding road leading to the amphitheater. After crossing the railroad tracks, they saw the Chateau De Mores rising from the empty plains a short distance away. Rosalinda's

second great-uncle had built it as a hunting lodge and summer home when he first established the town. When his ambitious business venture failed, the family abandoned the property, returning to their home in France, though they retained ownership of the estate.

As they continued past the chateau and began ascending up the road that curved around like a snake, as it led to the theater's parking area, Rosalinda announced, "I would very much like to visit there before we leave," which startled the group. Not because she wanted to view the chateau, but because she mentioned leaving. Charles could only hope it was a good sign she was ready to move forward with their life.

Paris beckoned him. He had put so many projects on hold when he made the decision to bring his wife here, not knowing how long they would be gone. He had chosen a script he wanted to produce months ago and needed to meet with his staff to develop the plan and obtain the financial backing for the production.

Regardless of what needed to be done, he did not regret putting his work on hold. Rosalinda held his heart, and he would always put her first.

Parking the vehicle, the two couples joined hundreds of others making their way across the open prairie toward the gate leading to the stage area. Steps had been cut into the hill to allow the audiences safer footing to the seating area. The climb back up could prove difficult for anyone who wasn't in good health.

The seating consisted of nothing more than rows of wooden benches without back support. They didn't look comfortable enough for a dog, but they were something to sit on. The two couples hunkered down to wait for the production to start.

"Excuse me," came a quiet, shy voice from behind Rosalinda, causing the starlet to turn to see a young teenage girl sitting behind her. "I'm sorry, ma'am, but has anyone ever told you that you look exactly like Rosalinda Vallombrosa? She's a famous actress from France."

"Betty!" the woman next to her exclaimed in embarrassment and apologized to Rosalinda. "Forgive her. I thought I taught her better manners than that!"

"But mom!" the girl wailed, "She looks just like her!"

Rosalinda could not explain the emotion that went through her. She had been recognized, and the girl seemed not to notice the scar. Could it be? Perhaps her fans would not care if there was an imperfection?

She was not a shallow woman, but she had feared the small disfigurement she could not hide would cause people to run in terror.

This surprising encounter helped her to remember how much she loved the spotlight and her fans.

She couldn't help herself. She beamed. "Yes," she smiled at the girl. "I am Rosalinda." She nodded toward Charles, seated at her left side. "But I am Rosalinda Lafayette now. This is my husband, Charles…,"

The teenager goggled. "Oh…My…God!" she squealed and looked at Charles. "I know who you are! You make movies! Movies with Rosalinda! I cannot believe it! I love your movies! I went to your movie, Love in the Spring, probably ten times with my best friend, Nichol and…,"

"Betty!" Her mother exclaimed, embarrassed to death.

"But mom!" The girl looked at Rosalinda and told her, "I have seen every single one of your movies! You are so talented! And I have a few of your photos taped to my wall!"

"Betty!" her mother again.

"Well, I do. Isn't she gorgeous? Gosh, can I have your autograph? My friends are going to be so jealous! They are never going to believe me!"

Charles motioned to the small camera strapped to the mother's wrist. "Perhaps a picture?"

Again, the girl squealed, "Oh…My…God!"

"Betty," this time, it was a sigh from the mother who knew a lost cause when she saw it.

"I would be happy to do so." Rosalinda stood up, moved into the small isle while the teenager did the same; a bounce in her step as she rushed down to stand next to the petite woman who wasn't much taller than herself at five-foot-four.

Pictures were taken, as there was more than one because the mother lost all embarrassment and declared she should be in on a picture as well. Her neighbors would be green with envy once they saw it.

When the photoshoot ended, everyone settled back into their seats as the show began.

Snuggling into Charles's embrace, Rosalinda watched the performances with a little bit of melancholy, remembering her passion for the stage, and missing it more than a little.

She glanced at Charles, whose eyes were on the stage, no doubt looking for flaws or things he would have done differently if he were running the show. He had been clean-shaven all the years she had known him, but now he was sporting a stubble of a goatee and a mustache. He was going to keep that look if she had any say in the matter. Bald or not, he was sexy as hell. How had she gotten so lucky? This man loved her in ways she had never thought possible. He sacrificed so much just for her. He remained by her side despite the trauma she had gone through, and even more telling was the fact he did not force or bring up the subject of the sexual relationship they had yet to begin. He was giving her time to heal, even knowing she might never want to perform the physical act ever again because it could trigger those horrible memories.

She was ready to make new memories with him.

Intermission arrived before she realized it was happening.

Colten stood. "I need to excuse myself for a moment. I'll be right back."

Charles also stood. "If you are heading to a privy, I would not mind joining you."

Jacqueline laughed as the two walked away, joining the growing numbers, also heading in that direction. "And men joke about women going in pairs."

Rosalinda was looking toward the stage. Did she dare?

"Are you listening to me?" Jacqueline asked. "Are you enjoying the show?"

"What?" Distracted, she turned toward her friend and blinked.

"You seem to be thinking about something. What is it?"

She leaned in and whispered her plan into her friend's ear. Though it was a wildly outlandish idea, she wanted to attempt it. She felt compelled to give Charles something special that came directly from her heart, believing he deserved the gesture after all his sacrifice.

Jacqueline laughed with delight. "Oh my gosh! That is a wonderful idea. I will keep the men distracted. You go turn on the charm, and I doubt they will say no to a famous relation of the Marquis de Morès."

Without delay, and a smile on her face wider than the state Rosalinda moved toward the stage.

As the men returned to their seats the lighting was being dimmed. The sun was dropping below the horizon, causing shadows to lurk in different areas of the arena.

"Where is Rosalinda?" Charles asked as he looked around, trying to see through the sizable crowd. He held a bag of popcorn and a soda in his hands from the concession stand. He felt like he had stood in line for hours to purchase them.

"She'll be back," Jacqueline promised. "She needed to use the ladies' room."

Charles blinked. Rosalinda was by herself? In a crowd?

It was happening all over again.

Panic overtook his thoughts. He hadn't realized until that moment the depth of his own anxiety that she could be taken from him once again.

Jacqueline stood up and moved to his side. "Charles, she's safe here." She understood his fear and could not blame him for it. "More importantly, she feels safe here. Enough so that she wanted to do something on her own."

Charles swallowed as he felt his heart thump with some feeling he could not explain. Knowing that Rosalinda had made the decision to wander through this crowd without an escort perhaps meant she had taken another step towards recovery.

Dare he hope?

"She better hurry," Colten said, "The show isn't going to wait for her to return before it begins the second half of the entertainment."

As though to emphasize the statement, the announcer walked onto the stage. He moved to the microphone sitting in the middle of the platform and raised his hands in the air. "Ladies and gentlemen," the man's voice boomed over the audience through the loudspeakers. "Normally, in this part of the show, it would be time to present our juggling act, but for now, we are moving that incredible performance to later in the show. Tonight, we have a very…very…special guest for you!"

Charles slowly sat down; his eyes riveted on the stage. His heart seemed to know...could it be?

Was she ready to be on stage once more and face an audience to preform?

He prayed his suspicion was true.

The announcer's voice thundered, "Ladies and gentlemen, direct from Paris to our humble stage we present- Rosalinda Vallombrosa!"

There was a collective gasp of excitement from the spectators, and then their applause echoed off the foothills of the badlands.

From behind the stunned Charles, young Betty called out, "She is Mrs. Charles Lafayette now!"

"Betty!"

Charles heard none of it. Time seemed to stop as he watched his wife, still wearing the pair of jeans and long sleeve plaid shirt she had arrive in, walk out from behind one of the building props on the far left of the stage.

She was the most glorious sight he had ever seen.

Without a word, Rosalinda walked to the microphone, smiled at the announcer then watched the man walk off stage before giving a nod to the band staged on her right.

The piano player immediately began the softly played beginning of Unchained Melody.

With the first note, her eyes went directly to Charles. As she sang the meaningful words from the song, she could feel the tears roll down her

cheeks. Her voice sounded like an angel singing from heaven up above, causing many in the audience to feel their own tears flow to the surface as they listened in awe. Not only was the song a beautiful declaration of her love for Charles, but her touching vocals grabbed the hearts of all in attendance.

Rosalinda was not aware of the new fans she was creating as she sang. In that moment, nobody else existed, she only cared that Charles would understand how much she loved and wanted him. This man, her husband, someone she had pushed away for years, because of her own foolishness, was her lifeline.

She doubted if any other man would have been as kind and gentle and patient under the same circumstances. If not for him being who he was, she knew she wouldn't have survived these past months.

Mesmerized by the words, Charles slowly stood to his feet, unconscious of his actions as if his wife had cast a spell on him. He was unaware when Jacqueline had taken the popcorn and soft drink from his hands.

The song was coming to an end.

Charles moved to the aisle and walked down the steps toward the stage.

Reaching the bottom of the platform, he climbed the five steps toward his wife. Oblivious to the fact that the women in the audience were sighing as they watched the romance unfold.

As the last notes of the song faded, Charles strolled across the stage to his wife, reached out to take her in his arms before kissing her with all the love and passion he held for her.

His own eyes were misty as he told her softly, "I love you beyond words."

The microphone picked up every word.

The audience roared their approval, and as the Lafayette's left the stage to find their seats, the applause that accompanied them took a long time to fade.

Chapter Twenty-Two

The drive back to the ranch was perhaps the longest trip Charles had ever endured. Watching Rosalinda singing a love song to him, in that beautiful come-hither voice, unhinged him. Now having her next to him in the car's backseat, snuggled up to him with her arms wrapped around him, her head resting on his chest and knowing the tightness in his loins would not go away was driving him mad. He had no idea how he would make it through this night, lying entwined but not sexually active.

God save him.

The moment Colten slowed the vehicle down in front of the Fisher home, Charles opened the door and shot out. With a quick look at his wife, God, she was beautiful, he murmured, "You run along to bed, darling. I have…." What Charles? -think! "Colten wanted to show me something in the barn."

Colten's brow raised. "I do…?" He saw the plea in Charles's eyes and said enthusiastically, "I do! Yes, of course. I forgot."

Charles didn't give anyone time to question anything; he began strolling toward the nearest building regardless of the fact it was not the barn. His thoughts bounced from, "I need a cold shower," to "Maybe I should get drunk." He needed some way to turn off the heat building up in his body. He had never wanted his wife more than he did on this night.

Jacqueline looked at Colten with a puzzled look, clearly wondering what was going on.

He shrugged as he smiled and kissed her cheek, "He's a greenhorn; can't remember which building is the barn. I best show him," and he moved away, following the path Charles had blazed to the machine shed.

Turning toward Rosalinda, Jacqueline said, "Poor man."

"I think he will feel better once he comes back," Rosalinda said and shared a secretive grin with Jacqueline before walking toward the guest

house. She was glad she and Charles had been staying there during their time here. The Fisher's had built the cottage not too far from the main house, but far enough for the privacy she wanted tonight.

She did not intend to sleep until the early hours of dawn.

Watching her best friend disappear into the front door of the guest house, Jacqueline chuckled, knowing precisely what was on the starlet's mind. She had her own plans for Colten this evening and hoped he wouldn't be too long in talking with Charles.

As for Colten, his thoughts mirrored his wife's, so when he entered the large building, which housed the largest equipment used on the ranch, he intended to nudge Charles along as quickly as possible. Seeing the Frenchman pacing alongside the tractor gave him pause. Obviously, the man was troubled.

"All right, Charles. What did you…"?

"Shoot me." Charles stopped in mid-stride and looked at him.

With a raised brow, Colten said, "Excuse me?"

"Shoot me, Colten. I cannot endure another minute."

"Umm…." Was all Colten could manage before the man began pacing once again. "Perhaps you would like to explain…."

Stopping, Charles looked at him intensely. "Do you have any idea how long it has been since I have had sex with my wife?!"

Again, "Umm…."

"I have never," Charles emphasized the word, "had sex with my wife!"

Colten almost laughed and would have if the situation was different. But he felt empathy instead of amusement, so he said nothing. What could one man say to the other when they had never been in the same situation? And now that Colten understood what the trouble was, he wasn't sure if there was anything he could say. Charles had already shown he was a man of integrity and loyalty. The fact he had stayed with Rosalinda through the trauma she suffered, never turning to another woman for his sexual needs, and putting Rosalinda's emotions first told the true tale of loyalty between husband and wife.

"I don't know what to say."

"I ache for her! Do you comprehend what I am saying? I have loved her for years. Years! I never believed she could ever love me." He ran both of his hands over his bald head. "That night when she accepted my proposal," he gave a shaky laugh. "I thought I was dreaming. Then she agreed to marry me, right on the spot!" Another laugh. "It has been a nightmare ever since, and I do not know if that makes me an honorable human being or the biggest fool of them all!"

"You are the noblest man I have ever met," Colten said. "I don't know the answer, and to say it's going to take time would be a waste of breath because you already know that. Perhaps it's time you talked to her about it. It has been months. Her injuries have healed, and who knows, maybe she's ready too," his cheekbones shown with a blush he had hoped to avoid. Joking around with his fellow man about sex and encouraging the act was a whole different ballgame.

He shook his head, cleared his throat. "I think you should talk to her about it," he repeated for lack of anything else.

"What if she says no?" Charles asked, voice hesitant.

Proper or not, Colten threw back his head and laughed. He was sorry for it, but what the hell. He had needed the humor to give this conversation some normalcy. "I don't think you would be any worse off than you are now," he chuckled.

Charles stared at him, but his lips smirked.

"Go on," Colten encouraged and tried not to feel guilty knowing his own wife would be waiting for him in their bed with open arms.

Feeling his heart racing in his chest, Charles moved past his friend and headed toward the little cottage. Just before he turned the knob on the front door, he murmured a prayer under his breath. Not that he expected anyone to hear him. He had never believed in God, but sometimes it seemed fitting to voice a request on the off chance someone might be listening.

She was not in the small living area. She was probably in bed. It was late, almost midnight, so when he opened the door to the bedroom and discovered she wasn't there, his mind halted for a moment, perplexed. Where else could she be at this hour?

Before he could wonder farther at his questions, the bathroom door opened behind him. Opening his mouth to tell his wife he wished to discuss the subject of the marriage bed, he turned around, gawked, and swallowed his tongue.

She stood there wearing a black negligee so shear it might as well not have been there. That glorious raven black hair of hers falling behind her back as though it were a cape. The smile she gave him was seductive and erased everything from his mind.

His erection was instant.

She advanced toward him with a soft sway to her hips. Without a word, she pressed herself against him, drew his mouth to hers, but she didn't stop her forward motion. He involuntarily was moved back while her lips were fused with his until the back of his knees hit the mattress and caused him to fall back. In turn, she lost contact with his mouth, but she held on to his neck and followed him down, unbuttoning his shirt as she went.

"I love you," she whispered in his ear, licked his neck.

Impatient to feel his flesh under her palms, she tore at the buttons of his shirt; they gave with a pop and bounced to the floor.

"Rosalinda!" he hissed, passion seizing him in ways he had never known.

She leaned down, kissed him deeply, dueled with his tongue. "I love you, Charles." She stroked his face, his chest. Looking up, she met his copper-colored eyes. "I believe I have always loved you." She slid her hands down, down. Reaching the waistband of his jeans, she loosened the belt, unzipped the fly, and cupped him with her hand. His erection begged for freedom, and she obliged.

"Oh God," he said as she slid down his body, and her tongue began to lick.

He closed his eyes, prayed he wouldn't erupt. It had been far too long since he had had sex. His body trembled, terrified he would disappoint her, but wanting the release. He groaned. He was on the edge. Ready, so ready.

161

"Not yet," she said and pulled her mouth away.

He almost wept.

She moved up his body, slowly. Stroking, licking.

"Rosalinda!" Reaching for her, she shook her head.

"I want to show you…" her voice cracked. Tears in her eyes, she told him, "I want to show you how much I love you. You are my heart. My soul. I never dreamed anyone could love me as much as you do."

Meeting her eyes, he reached for her face, used his thumb to wipe the tear that escaped. "Darling, you are my everything. Please, do not cry."

"I weep for all the wasted years I could have spent with you."

"Let tonight be the new beginning. No regrets. Know only that you will forever be my very breath." He found her breasts through the fine material, worked the nipples between his thumb and index fingers, and when she leaned in, he raised his head and suckled one through the lace.

She arched her back as she felt the warmth of his mouth move through her entire body. She wanted him. Too impatient to remove any more clothing, she raised her body up to slide him inside.

They both gasped, savoring.

Leaning forward once more, she took his mouth with hers, stroking his tongue as her hips began to move on him.

Bracing her hands on his chest, her movement became quicker, quicker until they both reached release together.

She collapsed on top of him, his arms going around her. The wonder and beauty of their union staggered. For the first time in both of their lives, it felt as though they were exactly where they were meant to be. They would be strong in the years to come. Together they could over-come whatever else life might throw at them.

Neither of them knew when they fell asleep, but when they began to stir, Charles took his turn, making slow love to his wife. Lazily kissing and licking her body where every scar had been formed. So, help him, God, he would create memories for his wife that would overshadow the horror she had endured.

When they were spent, neither of them having the strength to move, they curled into each other and slept undisturbed until noon. When the sun was at its peak, she stirred and found comfort in being wrapped in his arms.

Charles awoke before her, kissed the top of her head. "Did you sleep well?"

She rose from the pillow and kissed him. "Oh, yes." She lay back down, stroking his arm, not anxious to leave his side, but there was something she had to know. "Charles…. Are you...Sure?" She did not want to bring the subject up after their unforgettable night together but did not feel she could wait any longer. "Could you really love this baby?" It wasn't easy. She paused, nervously biting at her bottom lip. "I do not know how you could want this child when I do not know how or if I ever can truly love it the way a baby deserves to be loved."

His arms squeezed around her. "I love children. I have always known I wanted to be a father someday, and regardless of how it came to be, it is innocent. I can be its father, Rosalinda, because… because it is a part of you." Now it was his turn to move so he could look into her eyes. "I do not know what to say except this. If you can think of it as my child, I know you will love it with all your heart. No one needs to know the truth. It could have been easily conceived on our wedding night or before, it is our business, and frankly, anyone who dares to question it can go to hell."

Her heart hammered. She was frightened and yet-

Together. They could perhaps do this.

She was silent for a moment, finding the will, the determination.

"I have something to tell you," she said, and she would make it be the truth in her heart.

"What is it?" He smiled, stroking her cheek.

"You are going to be a father."

He paused, looked into her eyes. Smiled. "I love you," he whispered, understanding her resolve to birth a child who hadn't been conceived in love, but who would be loved.

She returned the smile, though it wasn't radiant. They could only take each day as it came, and she hoped she could have the courage she would need. "And," she told him, "It is time to go home."

"To Paris?" he clarified.

Now she did laugh. "I do not believe we live in Australia, dear heart."

He shook his head, chuckling at her humor. "When would you wish to leave?" He tried to keep the excitement from his voice, but he longed for the streets of Paris. Visiting here, he discovered a quiet beauty that would become a retreat for them when life in the spotlight became too much. However, there was still a certain appeal to the glamour of fame.

"Tomorrow?"

"Yes. It will be enough time for our pilot to ready the airplane."

Her rock, her everything, could do anything.

Chapter Twenty-Three

When they reached Paris, the warm afternoon sun shone as if it were welcoming them back home. Charles's chauffeur was waiting for them. "Do you wish for me to drive you home immediately, sir?" he asked, loading the last of the luggage into the trunk of the limo.

Turning to his wife, Charles said, "No. I wish to show Rosalinda something first." He had thought about it during the long hours of the flight.

She smiled. "What…?"

"You have to wait, dear heart." He opened the door of the limousine himself, allowing her to step in first.

It wasn't long before the chauffeur was driving on a road that wound around past the Eiffel Tower, leading to a construction site. Some workers were busy using bulldozers and heavy equipment as they cleared rubble, while others were erecting new structures. When their black Rolls-Royce rolled to a stop outside of the construction zone, the driver opened the door for them to get out. Taking his wife's hand in his, they began to stroll along the fence, watching the construction.

"I wanted to show you the new backlot for Lafayette Productions." He gestured to the large wooden sign announcing to the city what the future held for what was once fifteen city blocks. A billboard stood, announcing the production company with the company logo, a circle outlined in purple, depicting the world housed within. At the center of circle was a vibrant red rose. "We will make many movies here, Rosalinda, and so will others."

She looked at the logo and asked, "Why did you choose that symbol to represent your company?" She had always wondered but never asked the question.

His eyes sparkled, and he smiled, "Because it represents you."

She stared at him, and for a moment, he felt embarrassed by the truth. "The purple ribbon symbolizes your royal blood, the rose in the center

is for your name, and it covers the world because I want every country to know who you are."

With tears forming in her eyes, she leaned into him. They had not spoken about her returning to acting, although she ached to do so. But with the scar on her face and those on her body, she wasn't ready to show the world the evidence of her torture. When in public, she wore long sleeves to cover her arms and ankle-length skirts to cover her legs. She had adopted the side ponytail hairstyle to cover the left side of her face. She could not fathom how she would feel standing before a camera again, but the one thing she knew with certainty was she loved this man with all her heart. And although she hadn't been told, she knew this area was the abandoned neighborhood where Pierre took her, but everything was gone now. Nothing here would stir nightmares.

"Let us go home," she told him. Her fingers were still entwined with his, and together they reentered the Rolls-Royce.

"You may take us home now," Charles told the driver, exchanging a look with the man in the rear-view mirror.

"My pleasure, sir," the man said, and put the car into motion.

As the car maneuvered through the familiar streets, Rosalinda could not pretend she wasn't happy to be home. There was nothing like the excitement of Paris. But when the vehicle turned left instead of right on a road that should have led to Charles' chateau, she became perplexed. "Charles?"

"It is all right, darling. Not much farther."

"But…"

"Patience," he told her and motioned with his head, indicating the road ahead. Their driver turned through a secured gate that revealed a long-curving driveway leading to a 55,000 square foot mansion. The view took her breath away. Driving past many parked cars, the driver slowed to a stop as they reached the elegant iron front door. Suddenly the door of the elegant home opened from the inside and out-poured her entire family. Her parents and brothers, along with her sisters-in-law, nieces, nephews, and of course her new mother-in-law. Both of their mothers were crying, smiling, and waving all at the same time.

"Welcome home, darling." her husband said as he opened the door of the vehicle himself, exited and helping her out.

She stared at him before her eyes turned to scan the grand home in front of her. "What do you mean? This is not your chateau."

He shook his head. "I sold it, and your home as well, while we were in Medora. My chateau is now owned by a couple who raise poodles. We begin anew. This is our home, Rosalinda. Ours." He had wanted nothing in her life that could be a reminder of that horrific night. "I have always admired this home, and when it came up for sale, I had my solicitors obtain it and sell our separate residents. Our staff has worked day and night, moving our belongings and getting it ready for us before we returned. I hope you will be happy here."

She stared at him for a second and then threw her arms around him. "Oh, I love you! What a lovely surprise! I love it already, and I have yet to see the inside!" She was anxious to do so, but for a moment that would have to wait. Her family could not contain themselves any longer, as they showered her with hugs and happy tears; Overjoyed to have her back home in Paris.

When at last she was able to step into her new home, she was impressed with her husband's good taste in real estate. He could not have chosen a better home for them to start their new life together, he knew she would love it as much as he did. The splendid reception room opened into the breathtaking gardens, which were magnificent. The oversized master suite had a private bath and a walk-in closet, with beautiful etched sliding glass doors that opened onto a 1,431 square foot terrace. The view made her emotional as she thought about how blessed her life was. He had done so much for her, and she vowed to spend the rest of her life making him happy.

Her heart filled with joy upon seeing that his grand, exquisitely carved bed had been transferred from the chateau to their new home. It was perfect for the room they would share as man and wife.

Leaning into her husband she could not help herself as she whispered in his ear her mischievous plans for the coming night, and what she planned to do to him in that bed.

He wanted to demand everyone leave that instant, but managed to hold himself together, for the moment. Instead, he smiled down at her and kissed her with as much passion as the current audience would allow. He could tell by the softness in her eyes she was genuinely happy once again; he felt complete with her by his side. His wife, his lover, his friend.

On the second floor were four bedrooms. Each of them had their own terrace, although not as grand as the master suite. The entire home and garden were elegant and refined. She could not wait to fill their home with children.

The thought took her by surprise. She had not realized until that moment just how much she wanted children, and it was then it struck her that she truly wanted this baby. Suddenly she stopped walking as they toured the outdoor gardens, placing her hand on her stomach.

Concerned, Charles stopped by her side. "Are you well?"

She looked up at him and smiled. "Oh yes!" she exclaimed with a laugh. Instantaneously she spun around to face their small entourage of family gather in the garden with them. "We are having a baby!" she blurted.

A stunned silence greeted the news, but then cheers erupted, followed by congratulations. No one would question who the father was, all would assume Charles as the sire.

Charles' mother put her hand to her mouth and wept. "I am going to be a grandmother!" She had all but lost hope years ago when her son had not shown interest in any other woman, except the one he was now wed to. She thanked God he had heard and answered her prayers. She longed to hold a baby in her arms and was thrilled to see her son happy.

Later that evening, after the guests left for their own homes, Rosalinda took her husband's hand and led him to their room. With the skill of a seductress, she began slowly undressing while he watched. With her clothes peeled away, she moved toward him. She loved how he looked at her, never making her feel any less of a woman than she had once thought she was. Through his eyes, she felt perfect.

As she reached up to start unbuttoning his shirt, they heard voices from the other side of the door. "Sir!" The butler said firmly, "My employer has retired for the evening. I told you at the front door you can come back tomorrow…."

"I'm not going to be here tomorrow, and this is only a quick stop before I have to be back on the damn plane, so step aside or I'll move you myself."

Rosalinda could not help but laugh out loud at the scowl on her husband's face upon recognizing Cadman Benson's voice.

"His timing is impeccable," Charles griped, remembering the morning after his wedding, when in the process of making love to his wife for the very first time, they had been interrupted by the very same man while they were in this exact situation. "I have never been a violent man Rosalinda, but in this case, I believe I am going to punch him in the nose."

She slipped on a robe as she giggled, and her husband opened the door.

Cadman looked at Charles, then into the room. He smiled. "I'm not delaying anything, I hope." Of course, his tone suggested he wasn't sorry in the least.

"What do you want?" Charles asked, his own tone terse.

"Nice to see you too," the American said. "I only have about fifteen minutes before I have to get back in the taxi and head to the airport."

"Where are you traveling to?" Rosalinda asked as she came alongside her husband and finished tying the belt of the robe she'd put on.

He looked at her. "Egypt, but it's government business, so I can't tell you anything other than that." Motioning with his hand, he said, "Let's take this to your living room."

Rosalinda grew apprehensive. She tensed. Beside her, Charles put his arm around her shoulders, squeezed.

"Nice castle," Cadman commented on the new home as they made their way to the main living room.

"We like it," Charles took his wife's hand, to sit on one of the plush golden-colored couches with her. "What is this about? Do you have

169

news regarding Bellefeuille?" He hated having said the name, but it couldn't be helped.

Rosalinda shifted closer, wrapping her arms around her husband's waist.

"Unfortunately, that would be a no." Cadman shook his head. "The last intel I received reported that he's likely in Cuba. If so, there's no way to retrieve him from there. Castro doesn't play nice with any government." He looked at Rosalinda, sorry for the stress this caused her. "I know it's not a comfort, but I don't think he'll come back. Knowing him as I do, he'll consider he had his sick, perverted form of revenge and go after someone else. I won't promise this, but I believe you're no longer of interest to him."

She looked up at Charles, a tear forming in her eye, she feared for her unborn child. Perhaps she would be safe from Pierre, though she could never be certain, but what if he somehow discovered he had produced a child that night? Would he try to take it? Harm it? She had yet to give birth, but already she was protective of the baby.

Looking at Cadman, she took a deep breath and made the decision to tell him their secret, whispering, "I am pregnant."

Cadman blinked. He hadn't expected her to announce that after what he just said, but he told her congratulations anyway. But a glance at Charles, who shook his head slightly, gave him pause. When he comprehended her meaning, he cleared his throat. "Well, I don't know what to say."

"To the world, the child is mine," Charles told him. "Only a hand full of people know the truth, and obviously, my wife trusts you enough to tell you."

Clearing his throat again, Cadman could offer no promises except, "I will monitor Pierre's movement the best I can, and if I hear anything that suggests he might be coming your way, I will let you know. I wish there were more I could do except to say, keep yourself guarded but live your life."

Standing up, he glanced at his watch and knew he only had five minutes to finish this conversation. "Aimée-Louise," He shook his head

and amended, "Cynthia Payton, had no part in Pierre's plan, and I hope one day you will find it in your heart to forgive her."

Cadman had developed a friendship with the young woman as he helped her start a new life. The woman was currently enrolled in The Culinary Institute of America in New York. She was trying to discover for herself who she was meant to be without her mother ruling her life.

"As for Lilith," Cadman shrugged. "The old bat had a real heart-attack a few weeks ago and doctors weren't able to save her."

"May she rot in hell," Charles commanded.

"Amen to that," Cadman agreed. He walked to Rosalinda, taking her hand as he pulled her up. With the familiarity of an intimate friend, he lowered his head and kissed her on the lips. "Be happy, Rosalinda," he told her, then looked at Charles. "You'll answer to me if you don't treat her right."

With a laugh, Charles asked, "Would that be before or after her four brothers' have a go at me?"

Chuckling Cadman took his leave, on his way to Egypt, and only God knew what else.

Wrapping an arm around his wife's waist, Charles told her, "It is late. Let's go to bed."

"I hope you do not have sleeping in mind."

"It is the furthest thing from my thoughts."

"Good." They reached their bedroom once again, closing the door. Turning towards him, she began unbuttoning his shirt. "Now, where were we?"

Picking her up, he walked her to the bed and gently placed her there before stretching out on top of her. "Only at the beginning my love. Only the beginning."

Epilogue

Waddling, one could not consider it anything other than that, into Charles' home office, Rosalinda paused for a moment to rub at the cramp in her back. She honestly did not wish to disturb him. She knew he was busy revising a screenplay, but it couldn't be helped.

His back toward her, she moved forward, leaned in as much as her protruding stomach would allow, and wrapped her arms around his neck, kissing him on the top of his bald head. "Could you," she asked with a smile on her lips, "possibly drive me to the hospital?"

Distracted by the changes he was feverishly crossing out of the script he was reading, he mumbled, "If you could give me about an hour, I will be happy to take you anywhere you wish."

She felt another cramp begin, and road it out with her eyes closed. The contraction was not severe, but if they were a prelude to what was to come, she wasn't looking forward to the intense labor.

Feeling fluid seep down between her legs, she knew she probably did not have an hour to give. "It cannot wait."

He turned a page, "Hmmm."

She chuckled.

"Perhaps you can have our driver take you."

"To the hospital?"

"Certainly. You know he will take you wherever you wish to go."

"To the hospital?" she asked again.

He nodded, turning another page.

Smiling at his back, she tried not to laugh. He was not hearing what she was saying. "Do you think he will come into the delivery room with me as well?"

In the process of crossing out another line in the script, his hand stilled. Slowly, he placed the paper and pen on his desk as he turned to look at her. "Rosalinda, are you in labor?"

She nodded.

He sprang into action, calling out for Health to phone the hospital to let them know they were on their way.

"I already did that," Rosalinda assured him as he rushed around the room looking for God knew what. "And Dr. Brown will meet us there." He, along with one trusted nurse, would be the only medical personnel allowed in the delivery room. "What are you looking for?"

He stopped his frantic search. Looking at her with his eyes glazed. "I have no idea."

She didn't try to suppress her laughter.

"Are you laughing at me?" he frowned.

She shook her head. "Never."

"I think we should go to the hospital," he told her.

"I believe that is a wonderful idea."

Heath entered the room. "Your bags are in the car, Mrs. Lafayette, and the vehicle is at the front door. Godspeed. I cannot wait to have a little person running around here."

"Remember that when the child knocks over a vase," Patricia Lafayette told him as she entered the room, taking her son's hand. "This way, my boy, you are about to become a father."

He wanted to faint. All the months they had waited for this day to arrive, he felt confident, but now with the moment at hand, he could not deny he was nervous as hell. All his doubts and fears flooded his brain like a title wave, although he knew there was no turning back now, he panicked. Would he be a good father? Would he do right by this child? Would it know how deeply it was loved by him? If a day came that they had to reveal the truth about its true parentage, would the child turn away from him?

He vowed to be the best father a child could want.

Several hours later, he watched as Rosalinda give birth, holding her hand and encouraging her throughout the long labor.

Dr. Brown cut the umbilical cord, and the nurse cleaned and wrapped the baby. Then the woman brought Charles the bundle. Smiling, she asked, "Would you like to hold your son?"

He looked down at the infant and felt a lump form in his throat. His heart palpitating with excitement, he nodded. Holding the baby close, he walked over to Rosalinda. "We have a son," he told her, though his voice cracked. He was in awe of the little human life his wife had carried for nine months in her body. "You have given me a son!" He laughed as he brushed a finger over the softness of the newborn's cheek.

Rosalinda reached out her arms, anxious to see the bundle he held. When at last Charles placed their son in her arms, she took in the wisps of fine black baby hair. His eyes weren't open, so she had no idea what color they were. When he moved his face toward her breast, looking for nourishment, she doubted she had ever been so happy in her life. She had made the decision to give birth to him, and nothing could ever take her love away.

"And so, what is the young man's name?" Doctor Brown asked, moving in to look down at the cleaned-up infant.

"Mason," Charles answered. "Mason Richard Fernando Antoine Albert Lafayette."

"Well," Doctor Brown commented, "That certainly is a mouth full." Poor kid.

"He is named after Rosalinda's great-grandfather Richard, Duc de Vallombrosa. He founded the Yacht Club of France and the Society of Racing in Cannes."

"Fernando was the name of my father." Charles looked at Rosalinda, and he could see she understood his need to honor the man who had accepted him as his own. "Antoine for Richard's firstborn and, of course, Albert for her father."

With a shrug, the Doctor shook his head. The child was the one who would have to live with it, not him. "In a few hours, after you had a chance to rest, I will begin to allow your family to visit you." He rolled his eyes; he knew the waiting area was already overrun with the Vallombrosa family. "The hospital is also slowly being surrounded by your

fans," he told Rosalinda. "You might not have been on stage for a year, but they are still loyal." With that statement, he left the couple alone to enjoy the newborn in peace.

Charles sat down on the bed, watched his wife feeding their son, and wondered if there had ever been a more beautiful sight.

"Dear heart," Rosalinda said, she too could not take her eyes away from the baby's face. "What is the screenplay you are working on?"

Distracted, he said, "It is a mystery drama."

"Have you cast the leading lady yet?"

"No. I have not found any one right for the part."

She looked up at him, smiling as she batted her eyes. "Perhaps I might know someone if you would give her an audition. Perhaps you know her? She has been cast in numerous plays and even a few of your movies. I believe her acting abilities may have won your last film some awards."

His heart drummed. "You wish to return to the screen?"

"Well, if I knew a director who knew how to block a shot and would allow me to wear long sleeve tops…."

"You are hired!" he exclaimed, kissing her. "I wanted you for the part, but…" he trailed off. They both knew why he hadn't asked.

"You have me now, darling. Now and forever, I am yours."

Author notes

This story is a work of fiction based on historical facts. Although some events may not have taken place in the exact time frame of the story.

While researching the history of the town of Medora, I went through the genealogy of Antoine-Amédée-Marie-Vincent Manca de Vallombrosa, the Marquis de Morès, and his wife, Medora Von Hoffman Vallombrosa, Marquise de Morès. Once a person looks back far enough, sometimes a story can be told that weaves history and fiction together.

Richard, Duc de Vallombrosa, who married Geneviève de Pérusse des Cars, did found the Yacht Club of France, and the Society of Racing, in Cannes.

Richard and Geneviève's descendants are as follows: Antoine-Amédée-Marie-Vincent Manca de Vallombrosa, the Marquis de Morès was their firstborn. Six years later, a son, Odet, was born. However, he only lived for a few months. In 1868, a daughter, Claire, was born. Then, in 1880, another son, Amédée, was born. (Amédée Joseph Ga-briel Marie Manca-Amat de Vallombrosa was a French organist and composer.)

When I discovered Richard and Geneviève's son, Odet, had not lived, I wondered what his family line would have been, had he survived. That is where the imaginary line of the Vallombrosa family begins. I felt Odet deserved to have his own Legacy, and this is from where Rosalinda was born. The fabricated family line is— Odet, born 1864, Victor, father of Albert, and Albert, father of Rosalinda.

Medora Vallombrosa was a daughter of Athenais Grymes von Hoffman and Louis A. von Hoffman, a New York banker and one of the founders of the Knickerbocker Club. Medora's maternal grandparents were Susanna Bosque Grymes, third wife and widow of William C.C. Claiborne, the first American Governor of Louisiana, and John

Randolph Grymes, the United States Attorney for Louisiana, and personal counsel to Andrew Jackson, during the Battle of New Orleans. He resigned from his post to represent the pirate Jean Lafitte. Medora was named for her maternal aunt, who was the second wife of Samuel Ward, acclaimed Washington lobbyist, whose first wife was Emily As-tor, daughter of William Backhouse Astor. Ward's sister, Julia Ward Howe, wrote The Battle Hymn of the Republic.

Researching Medora's mother's family tree was interesting. I was amazed by the connections to other famous people in history. When forming Jacqueline's link to Medora, North Dakota, I went through Medora's mother's line to bring it forward.

If you have never visited Medora, ND, I encourage you to put it on your bucket list. It is full of history, and the scenery is breathtaking

One final note: De Morès's last name was not Vallombrosa; Manca was. De Vallombrosa was a title which I took liberties with.

About the author

J.R. Zimmer is an artist and writer.

Author of the Fisher/Lafayette Series.

J.R. Zimmer was born in Bismarck, North Dakota, in 1960. (Good lord she's getting old) She has been enthralled by the badlands since the first time her parents took the family there when she was five years old.

The Fisher/Lafayette Series was born from her enchantment with the historical figures Antoine-Amdée-Marie-Vincent Manca de Vallombrosa, the Marquis de Morès, and his wife, Medora.

You can find J.R. Zimmer at:

Web site: www.jrzimmer.com

Email: jrzimmer17@yahoo.com

Keep Reading for an expert of Book Three in the Fisher/Lafayette Series: Someone Like You

Someone Like You
by J.R. Zimmer

Chapter One

Most days, Cadman Benson was in a good mood.

Today was not one of them.

As he climbed into his 1975 Black Pontiac Firebird, he considered telling the President of the United States to take the job and shove it up his ass. It would not have been the first time he had had the same thought in his eleven-year career.

Had the task force not recently completed a successful hostage-rescue mission in Iraq?

Yes, they had.

Did the American people know this had happened?

No, they did not. Why? Because according to the government, the team did not exist. It was part of a confidential organization that only a few select officials knew about. The fewer people involved, the easier the secret was to keep, which was key to the team's success and of course, deny ability.

But it sure would be nice if the president would thank the team occasionally instead of reprimanding him when things went wrong. Like the incident involving the helicopter and the power lines in Eilat. They had no choice but to engage the kidnappers when they tried to fight back.

Sure, the team lost a helicopter, but more importantly, the team was successfully able to extract all the hostages, including that goddamn Senator, who now claimed he suffered trauma during the extraction and was demanding someone pay.

Pay for what? Saving his dumbass?

Stupid shit.

The man shouldn't have been in Iraql in the first place, knowing it was never stable enough for anyone to be there.

Cadman started the engine as he contemplated kidnapping the Senator in question and delivering him back into the hands of the ones who had

abducted him in the first place. Perhaps the man would rather be "traumatized" by them.

Those people wouldn't handle the pussy with gentle hands.

Shit head.

Placing the car in reverse, Cadman jettisoned out from the parking space. Knowing he should have looked first, before hearing, "Fucking A! Watch where you're going!" being screamed at him.

Cadman did not care. He didn't bother to stop the vehicle or apologize. He slammed the gear shift into drive and shot forward out of the White House parking lot.

"Your team should have been more careful," President Ford said. "The Senator wants heads to roll."

Whatever.

Ford could soothe the Senator's ruffled feathers, and this would all wash under the bridge, but damn it, men had risked their lives for that whinny son-of-a-bitch!

Perhaps the fact this was an election year had something to do with Cadman's added frustration. Not knowing who would be elected and then ultimately become the new leader of Task Force Ghost always put him in a foul mood.

Ford was the third president to have the responsibility to give directives to the task force since it first formed in 1965 under Lyndon B. Johnson.

Johnson had put this group of elite commandos together after Congress passed the Gulf of Tonkin Resolution in 1964. It granted Johnson the power to use military force in Southeast Asia without having to ask for an official declaration of war.

Officially Cadman handpicked the members. President Johnson handpicked him to lead the best of the best men that would be-come Task Force Ghost.

Cadman had been a Secret Service agent for eight years before Johnson offered him the position to head up the special op. Before that, he had been a twelve-year Marine. With thirty-one years of service to the United States under his belt, he was not worried about a Senator who had been 'traumatized.'

But it pissed him off to have the president bitch about it instead of thanking the team for getting all the hostages back safe and sound.

Cadman pointed his car in the direction of the mall, intending to pick up a new down-filled vest. There was a sale on today at one of the department stores, and he needed a new one since his one-year-old German shepherd had taken it upon himself to use his last one as a chew toy. Besides, maybe taking some time to look through the clearance racks would help him put this whole thing from his mind and calm him down.

Perhaps Ford would lose the election, and the next president would be more appreciative of the men's efforts.

Thinking about who the potential candidates were would only give him indigestion if he were to dwell on it. He figured Ford would probably get the Republican endorsement; however, if that happened, Cadman would not be happy with the choice. Perhaps it was wrong to hope your current boss would be out of a job, but Cadman had never been a fan of Ford.

However, out of respect for the office of the Presidency, Cadman largely avoided questioning the orders from the person holding the position. Besides, if Ford was re-elected, there was much to be said for the expression: better the devil you know than the one you don't. A new President always meant an unsettling adjustment period for the White House staff and those under the president's command.

As far as Cadman was concerned, the democrats running for their party's nomination weren't much better than Ford.

As the mall came into view, Cadman pushed thoughts of the election from his mind; there was no point thinking about something he couldn't control.

3

He found a parking space opening that was close to the main entrance of the shopping center. At least something was going right for him today.

With any luck, he'd find a vest in no time and be on his way home…

As he was exiting his car, he suddenly remembered the promise he'd made his mother three months ago: to stop by her house today and put up the shelves in her bedroom. "Damn it!" he thought. Why couldn't he have remembered that before leaving the house this morning so he could have grabbed the tools he needed on his way out?

Knowing his mother would likely disown him if he canceled yet again, he resolved to stop at the hardware store on the way to her place and buy the necessary items. He was in no mood to drive across town to his own place for tools, only to backtrack to her house. At least this way, he could leave the new set at his mother's, just in case some unexpected "Honeyboy" projects popped up down the road.

With a resigned sigh, he walked into the mall, hoping to find a down vest on sale that fit his 6 foot, two-hundred-pound frame. It didn't really have to be a bargain price. He had funds. The government paid him well, but he enjoyed finding good deals.

As he was looking through the racks of vests, pulling one out to try on, he heard a voice from behind him say, "Good god, Benson. I thought for sure you never ventured beyond your office or otherworldly activities."

Cadman turned and grinned at the man standing on the other side of the clothing rack.

Gary Davidson was one member of the force, a local operative who worked as a mechanic at the Last Stop Garage when not needed for a mission. All the men in the unit, except Cadman, maintained civilian jobs to keep a low profile and blend with the public. Cadman strategically had his operatives spread across several states rather than clustered together. When he wasn't organizing a mission, Cadman spent his weekdays in an office building near the White House. His job was to monitor the world's illegal activities and prepare his specialized team to step in when the regular military could not handle the situation.

Taking the vest, he'd tried on off, he grabbed another one from the rack and slipping it on, as he told Gary, "I get out of my hole once in a while. Sometimes I frequent a grocery store too."

Laughing, Gary put a hand over his heart and said, "Be still my heart! You mean, you eat?"

They bantered back and forth until Cadman located the vest he wanted. "Nice chatting with you," he said to Gary, quickly adding, "I have an appointment." He saw no reason to elaborate that the appointment was only his mother waiting for help.

"Sure," Gary said, understanding Cadman's excuse to leave, but he still fell into step with him as Cadman made his way toward the checkout counter. "By the way," Gary added casually, "what did your boss say about that job we did for him?"

Cadman stopped, turned toward him, and refused to make this guy's day into a downer.

"He was happy as a clam."

Gary grinned ear-to-ear. "That's great! What did he say about the bird?"

"That part he wasn't pleased about, but those things happen."

No point mentioning that Ford was considering having the Ghost Team pay for its replacement out of their paychecks over the next ten years. Finding money to replace equipment destroyed by a team that didn't officially exist was nearly impossible. The Ghost Team was not listed in any government budget under anything relating to the military. Instead, those in charge hid the necessary funding in legislative bills marked for entirely different causes—a classic trick. The government loved stashing budgets inside bills that Congress would pass without batting an eye, knowing full well no one ever read them thoroughly.

The two men started walking again. Reaching the checkout area, Gary paused to snatch a magazine, then nudged Cadman. "See that?" he said,

tapping the cover image. "She could definitely make a guy forget his troubles!"

Half-expecting Gary to be pointing at Farrah Fawcett, the actress who had men across the United States lusting over her in the new television series Charlie's Angels, Cadman was shocked to see he was wrong. He was even more surprised when Rosalinda Lafayette's cat-like green eyes stared out at him from the cover of the magazine. The headline read: "Rosalinda! French Actress Expecting Second Child, Eleven Years After Giving Birth to Her Son."

Gary paged through the magazine until he found the story. "Can you believe it? Wow. I can't believe she would wait that long to have another baby."

Cadman wanted to shut down the conversation about Rosalinda immediately. He knew the heartache she and her husband had endured over the years, desperately wanting a house full of children, only to face the reality that Rosalinda might never have more than one. Cadman knew the Lafayettes personally; in fact, he was an honorary uncle to the boy, loving eleven-year-old Mason as though he were his own son. Regardless of the circumstances of Mason's conception, the child never lacked love. Cadman's mind flashed back almost nine months: he had been visiting the Lafayettes in Paris when Rosalinda burst into her husband's office, tears in her eyes, and announced she was pregnant.

It was an announcement that all of France wanted to celebrate. The country loved Rosalinda and her husband, Charles.

Cadman was determined not to reveal his connection to the couple. That was his private life, and he would guard it fiercely. He dismissed Gary's curiosity with a terse comment: "Gary, you're acting like a gossipy old woman."

With a hoot of laughter, Gary put the magazine back on the rack, much to Cadman's relief, and said, "Boss, admit it. She's gorgeous."

To himself, Cadman said, absolutely, but for Gary, he only shrugged. He wanted to be done with this conversation.

"No wonder you're not married," Gary grumbled under his breath.

Cadman chuckled. "I like women, but I don't need one in my life."

"Spoken like a die-hard bachelor."

Laughing, Cadman paid for the vest, said goodbye to Gary, and headed for his car.

The next stop was the hardware store, then his mothers.

He glanced at his watch. The teenager he hired to walk the dog a few times a day would have last been at the house about an hour ago. That would give Cadman a few hours to get those shelves up before the dog would need to be let out once more.

Why he had got a dog in the first place, Cadman wasn't sure. Perhaps for the companionship it offered. It was nice to come home and have the big lug greet him at the door. Thankfully, he had found a dog sitting service he could depend upon to take care of Mutt on short notice or when he had to leave on a mission that had him not knowing how long he would be gone.

Before leaving the mall, Cadman put the new vest on.

Not that the day was overly cold, but the wind had picked up, and thirty-seven degrees above zero would feel a lot more comfortable with the added protection.